MW01240844

FRACTIONS

FRACTIONS

TALES FROM THE UNIVERSE OF
ORDER'S LAST PLAY

E. ARDELL

JOVIAN EMPRESS
SAN JOSE, CA

All rights reserved. No part of this book may be reproduced or transmitted in any form or by any means, electronic or mechanical, including photocopying, recording, or by any information storage and retrieval system, without permission in writing from the author.

CONTENTS

FOREWORD

When writing a long series with multiple characters in each book, sometimes it's a little hard to squeeze in as many details as we'd like about everyone. There are so many things authors know about their worlds and characters that readers never will. The trend of creating novellas or books of short stories set in the universe of a series' is wonderful, and I am embracing it.

FRACTIONS is my first novella, a series of short stories about Evan Lauduethe and his close friends Adonis Maeve, Jalee Orcharest and Desiri Lilias that covers times before the events of the FOURTH PIECE, and scenes between THE THIRD GAMBIT and its upcoming sequel THE SECOND ENDGAME. These characters grew up fighting bad guys and working big magic while still managing to be kids and teenagers when allowed. Find out what it was like and be prepared to chuckle.

If you aren't caught up in ORDER'S LAST PLAY, check my website for more information or to sign up for my mailing list: EArdell.com

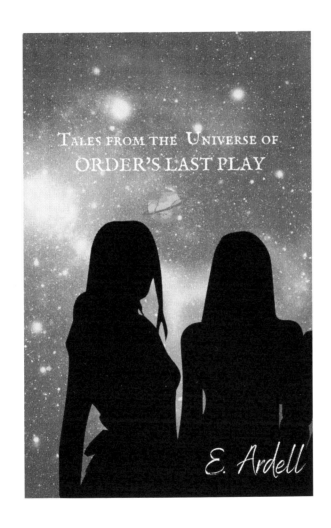

TALES FROM THE UNIVERSE OF
ORDER'S LAST PLAY

E. Ardell

THE TAMING OF THE CAT OWNER

Evan Lauduethe

"EVAN."

I jerk up, my fist shooting out to punch whatever's leaning over me. A strong hand catches my knuckles, then shoves me backward. The strength is surprising—for a *wisp*, then I crack open an eye. "Oh, it's you."

I let myself fall back into my pillows and roll onto my side, curling up. My inner time-keeper says that it's nowhere near time to be conscious. We're on leave; no early wake-up calls, no night raids, no emergency drills.

Adonis's presence continues to loom over me, unmoving. The weight of that granite stare of his keeps me from going back to sleep. I roll onto my back, glaring at him. "What?"

My flat-mate—best friend—cousin-by-marriage—first in command—*ashfug* keeping me awake—stands there, unblinking. "There's a creature in the kitchen."

"*Niobe-va*," I moan. "If it's another *fippin'* vribil, just nab it by its tail and *chug* it out a window. They know their way back to their box." The fuzzy little rodents are always getting out, but they're harmless. Adonis hates them because they're ugly. To me, they look like yellow Earth rats. Not the most endearing creatures, but vribils don't bite.

"It's not a vribil."

I frown at him. Adonis's Magic Breed heritage shows in the way his face usually lacks expression. Nymphs don't smile or blink much. Not many people can tell what he thinks or feels from his body language

6

alone, unless you're me. I've known him since we were five Common Years old. Right now, those gray pupil-less eyes glint with something that tells me I better go look in the kitchen, now, or he might kill me. And since I've never known Adonis to be dramatic, I get up.

"Fine." I shuffle after him as he leads me out of my room and towards the kitchen. Lights flicker on overhead as we move and I shield my eyes. The retired soldier who'd passed this place on to us didn't have night-vision. I can adapt my eyes to the light, but not fast enough to keep it from blinding me on night-trips to the kitchen. We really need to take the time to pull the setting manual up on our comp-als. I don't think either one of us knows how the stuff in this flat truly works. But we're here so seldomly that it kind of doesn't matter much.

The kitchen lights are on. The blue-white floors and walls gleam, courtesy of Adonis's neurotic cleaning habits. It helps that he's fast and his elemental affinity is water. Makes keeping things clean easy. I still think we should get a cleansing system, but he likes spending the minutes it takes him to scrub counters and floors, says it makes the place feel more lived in. We live more on the Ievisara—our warship—than here, but he doesn't take time to clean his designated quarters onboard.

Something growls and the sound of teeth tearing through containers and knocking over bottles and jars brings my sleepy eyes to the food bay. The big storage unit stands taller than me, its panels and doors as blue as the rest of the kitchen, as a large furry body rummages its shelves. A long, thin tail with a ball of fluff at its end wags, as the monster uses its paws to push things to the side and its tongue slurps up spilled liquid.

I blink and Adonis turns to look at me, perfectly god-like: dark olive-toned skin, symmetrical features, black hair, and nearly a foot taller. Everything about him is as condescending as the dumb name his parents gave him because they read too many mythromance novels before he was born. But you know what, I might be deserving of a little condescension right now, because...

"You're right. It's not a vribil."

He continues to stare at me.

"I'll... get it out of here and clean up."

A straight brow lifts. He hates the way I clean.

"Fine, then. I'll just get it out of here. And... order more food."

An audible breath through his nose signals his extreme annoyance, though his face remains calm and unreadable. Then, he leaves me alone with my latest acquisition without a backward glance.

"Tula, sweetness. I fed you before bed. There's no way you're hungry again." I chance my way to the riorfox I'd rescued from extermination. It had stowed aboard an inbound ship from the Cratperan Solar System in Sector Nine. Upon entrance in the shuttle bay, the big cat burst out and tried to eat a few porters before running through the meeting and training halls. Lots of yelling, lasic-fire and cursing occurred before someone grabbed me and had me corner it. I have a way with animals, and I'm completely against harming them.

They share our worlds with us; they feel, they breathe, they raise families. They're not beneath us, just different. "Tula." I hum a sweet song, the one that charmed her and brought her toward me in the meeting hall. The Hall of Decision became a temporary animal shelter when I'd ordered in a collar and leash and turned one room into a make-shift holding pin until I'd been ready to take her home. The Remasian Council had not been pleased with me, but what else is new? The Councilors are never happier than when they see my backside, leaving, rather than having me join discussions about political matters concerning our planet. I mean, why should I be there? I'm just the leader of the planet—the face and name the people bless. But I don't run the place, just fight the physical battles. And *Hades and Ether*, I don't even pick the battles.

The riorfox stops pawing through the unit, body shuddering in pleasure as I run my hand along her spine. Her fur's soft and silky, purple-black as the night sky, and warm. She goes down on all fours, putting her at waist level, and gazes at me. She's like a blend of several large Earth cats, a cheetah's head, a lion's mane, a tiger's powerful body, with a stuffed animal's tail. Liquid black eyes glitter as her head lolls from side to side with my song. Cat nip. That's what humans give cats to make them amiable, right? It's been a while, but I remember things about my old home, and even study to keep up with it. There's an old saying about taking kids out of a place, but not being able to take the place out of the kid. I'm half-human and, though I only lived on Earth for a few short years, I feel nostalgia for it.

"You've been a naughty girl," I purr to the riorfox. "You've made a horrible mess. I told you to stay in your box. I thought you understood."

Tula stares at me some more. I swear she gets it. Riorfoxes are smart. I did research to learn about feeding and grooming them. Found out Tula's still an adolescent, like me, and her breed itself is a unique mix of different feline species. Again, like me, a unique mix of DNA, human, Remasian, Magic Breed, Amphoran. No one really knows what to expect of our behavior and everyone doubts we can truly be tamed or trained.

But I don't want to tame nor train Tula. I'm working on scheduling transport, so that I can take her home and set her free. Wish somebody could do that for me. Not that I want to go back to Earth. I don't belong with humans, but I'd love to be free. I scratch behind one of Tula's long ears.

"Let's get you back in your box." I hum again, and start to walk, waiting to feel her at my back, and don't. I turn, eyeing the riorfox as she looks right back at me. "Come?"

A blink.

Maybe I need a treat or something, but she's already helped herself to all of the food. And—oh *fip*. Tula spins, sprinting out of the kitchen... and down the hall that leads to Adonis's room.

Well, I hadn't planned on dying tonight, but I suppose now is as good a time as any to plan my death ceremony. But first, I step over fallen jars and bottles, avoiding spilled juices and crushed fruits to see what's salvageable in the food bay. Die on an empty stomach? Not in this lifetime. The goddess would not be pleased.

I find an intact malibulg and hop up on the counter to peel it, while counting down the *wisps* to my doom.

Adonis never disappoints.

~*~

"THE NYMPH WAS IN RARE form this morning! He froze two of the new recruits," Desiri crows, laughing as I glare at her. "I'm guessing it's because of this thing. By the way, I told the troops you were supposed to be working with this morning that you were too busy styling your hair to show up for drills. I gave them a good work-out in your place."

The assassin mage crouches down to join me in the ankle-high, purple hacha grass. I lie on my stomach, elbows planted in soft dirt.

13

Chin propped in my hands, I study Tula, as she sits like a Sphinx ignoring me. We're practicing 'stay'. I slowly get to my feet. The grass sways, missing my close presence and I smile. I'd grown this grass from seed; it thinks I'm its mother. And, in a way, I am. The purple yard is sectioned off by silver rocks with areas for flowers, vegetables, shrubs, and fruit-bearing trees. The previous owner hadn't thought much of the growing space and let it go to *pidge*. The ground was nothing but cracked dirt, split by weeds, the barren trees sagged, leaves crispy and dead. Now, the yard thrives. Several vribils scamper through the grass, heading for the malibulg trees. Their plump bodies shimmy up the green-barked trees to get at the purple bulbs of fruit.

I take several test steps back, watching as Tula remains in place. I'd told her to stay moments before Desiri entered the garden. So far, so good. Tula remains in place as I nearly reach the side door that leads into the backroom I use as an animal shelter.

"Have I told you what a weird layout this

place has?" Desiri says. She gets up, following me to the side door. "Whoever heard of a sphere-shaped flat with a yard in the middle?"

"The architect was creative." I shrug. "He wanted his house to stand out in a crowd." All the other houses in the First Dome are rectangular with the yards on their outer edges. No trees, no flowers. Soldiers don't have time for shrubs and plants that need care.

"You picked this flat just to be weird," Desiri snorts. "You're becoming predictable."

"How inconsiderate of me," I say, opening the side door. Tula still lounges in the same spot. Good. I step inside, holding the door open for Desiri to follow and then curse, shoving Desiri to the side. Tula bounds toward the house, leaping through the door. She lands heavily, almost bowling me over. I nearly topple into the box holding the family of agor birds I saved from a tree in the Center Atrium of Shopping Square Seven. Seems folks don't like birds *pidging* on their heads while they're buying stuff. I usually let them loose in the yard, but I'm afraid Tula might eat them.

"I told you to stay!" I glare at the cat. Tula licks a front paw and stares at me.

Desiri snickers. "You know, you're looking a little rough there, *gak mopi*. Been at this long?"

"Most of the night, all morning," I grumble, eyes on Tula. "Stay."

"Maybe tell her to 'come' and you'll get what you want," Desiri suggests. I growl at her.

Tula lies down, watching me.

"I tell her to stay, she gets comfortable, like she's going to do it. See, not moving." I gesture to the riorfox.

I turn to Desiri, eyeing her full uniform, thick black work boots, cargo pants, full flack jacket open to reveal a tank top. Though I can't see them, I smell the different metals of half a dozen blades on her person and the magics she imbued them with.

"How many new transfers did you scare off?"

Desiri grins and tosses coppery brown curls over her shoulder. Her hair's longer than mine, falling to her waist, and held back by a couple of poison-laced hair pins. "Only two. Adonis scared off seven. Rare form, I tell you."

I flinch at that. "How many new transfers did we have?"

"Nine." Her grin widens. Her round, pretty face glows with mischief as her amber eyes gleam. "You won't miss them. They weren't good enough to be in our outer court. Let them join another field squad."

My personal guard is small, consists of three people, Desiri and Adonis being two of them. My outer guard could use a few more soldiers, but they all have to pass Desiri and Adonis's standards before we try them out. I trust them with that, though it's starting to seem like my outer guard will forever stay limited.

"Have you eaten yet?" I ask. "I ordered more food. The delivery should be coming in—whoa!"

I don't move fast enough to catch Tula as

she springs to her feet and lunges. I dodge out of instinct and realize my move is exactly what she wants. I was blocking the door to the rest of the flat. The thin metal door gives way as she crashes into it and becomes a furry streak of black and purple. I cringe as I hear furniture fall and glass break throughout the flat. A thought occurs to me.

Desiri's here, meaning practice is over, and she doesn't have the code to enter my flat by herself.

"Desiri, did you, uh, come home with Adonis today?"

We step into the living area. The frost that meets my feet, and coats the walls and windows, answers my question: Yes.

I groan. "Oh, come on! Again? I defrosted the place last night! You nearly killed the yard! It has to stay warm!"

Desiri laughs as I take a breath, dipping inward and stirring up my magic. The fiery stove in my belly where my magic lives heats my blood, raising my body temperature. I share it with the room, emitting heat from my pores. Frost and ice melt as I move around the living area. I increase the heat to turn puddles of water to vapor. I have to inspect the entire flat for ice now and make sure nothing's left wet or the place will reek for *cycles*.

Adonis appears in the doorway that leads out into the guest reception room. He stares at me.

"It leaves today," he says.

I blink. "No way. It'll be a week before any ships heading out to Cratperan dock here."

He folds his arms over his chest.

"There's nowhere else for her to go," I say. "No shelter is going to take a riorfox."

"There's a reason." Adonis's tone is cool.

"I know!" I say. "But I can train her." I can train just about anything.

Adonis narrows his eyes.

"I just need more time," I say, "and she'll only be here a few more *cycles*."

"Uh, Ev?" Desiri's voice is practically bubbly.

What's she so happy about? I turn to look at her, and she nods her head to the left, peering beyond me at something.

19

Dread fills me as I follow her eyes to Tula creeping into the living area with one of Adonis's shirts between her teeth.

Fip. My gaze goes back to Adonis whose gray eyes glitter with malice.

"I'll tame her," I say. "Give me a *cycle*. I'll get it done." And I must believe I can do it, because the words come out of my mouth easily. I can't lie, not even to myself. So, training Tula must be possible. I just have to figure out how, before I'm frozen out of my own flat.

"One *cycle*." Adonis shoots a dark look at Tula and his shirt. I yelp as my hands ice over, before he heads back to his room.

I thaw my fingers as Desiri cackles behind me. "Oh, *gak mopi*, are you ever in trouble."

I ignore her, making my way to Tula and snatching at Adonis's shirt. The riorfox clenches her jaw, holding on tight. I yank and she tugs back, ripping the shirt in two. I inspect the slobbery sleeve in my hand with a weary sigh.

"Don't suppose you'll help?" I say over my shoulder.

More laughter from Desiri, as Tula growls and goes back to shredding the remains of Adonis's shirt, long tail wagging.

I am in deep *pidge*.

~*~

RIORFOXES ARE NOT PETS.

Everything I read says it, everything Tula does proves it. The only thing that keeps her in one room is magical warding. I ward the yard to keep her outside when I'm not home and keep the other animals inside the shelter. It makes for angry creatures when I get back and reverse their positions: other creatures outside, Tula in.

I could just leave it at that. Ward her in, ward her out, give her food and clean water. It's only for a few more *cycles*, a ship will be here soon. Only, that's no way for anything to live. I don't run an animal prison. So, I let her out in the house when I'm home, but she's leashed. She forgets I'm stronger than her and she can't drag me around when my feet are planted.

Where I go, she goes: washroom, kitchen, work room, bed.

THE WASHROOM:

"Oi vati fipping pidge!"

I'm knocked against the bathing chamber wall by a giant ball of fur. Tula stands on her hindlegs, making her *iuts* taller as her black eyes gaze down at me. She presses her wet face against mine and licks my cheek. Her entire body doesn't fit in here with me if she goes down on all fours. Her puff-ball tail thumps against the clear plex-wall separating the chamber from the rest of the washroom and keeping the soap and water in.

I dance with a hairy partner as I struggle to get clean and avoid her tongue. Guess she likes the soap I make from my garden fruit. She certainly likes to eat the fruit, right off my trees. I groan, thinking about my poor, fruit-barren trees.

"*Fip*, that's my foot, big girl!"

I leave the bathing chamber with a soaking-wet, five-hundred *ium* riorfox on my back nibbling on my hair. I frown at fragments of a chewed-through Nokin-leather leash strewn over my bedroom floor. An expensive mistake.

THE KITCHEN:

"That's mine, you beast!"

Tula shoves her face in my porridge bowl, devouring my protein mix. Blue and yellow powder flecks her jowls and whiskers. I snatch my kava away from her, before she can swat it off the meal table with a paw. I hold my steaming cup in both hands, concentrating on its heat in an attempt to keep my temper. I grind my teeth.

She doesn't know better. She's wild. She likes protein powder. My protein powder. Because I poured another bowl just for her, but she ignored that one. I stare at the creature sitting next to me, hindquarters in the chair, back straight, just like a person.

I pick her bowl off the floor and set it on the table. She looks at me, then puts her face in that bowl too.

Huh. Maybe she just wanted to eat at the table.

I drink my kava.

THE WORK ROOM:

"No! Don't...!"

The Raz-skin leash snaps in two and I can't grab the cat before she knocks over a glass urn of holly powder. I dive for the urn. My middle finger brushes the base of the ornamented jar before it shatters on the rock floor. Holly powder puffs from the wreckage, igniting as soon as air touches it, filling the room with pungent, white spirit-smoke.

Fip. I jump to my feet, pulling at random wind melodies, needing a few gusts of wind

24

to funnel the spirit-smoke down into the floor vents, before—

The blood moss coating the ceiling for insulation shudders, reacting to the smoke. Tiny buds blossom, releasing fluffy pollen than drops right into the darien bowl on the mixing table. The one filled with kanja water, mir, podeli, and essence of mag—all very explosive when exposed to—

I throw up a quick-and-dirty energy field. *Fip*, this thing isn't going to set before—

The explosion takes out half my workroom.

I lie on the floor with a potion splattered riorfox on top of me, listening to the sound of an energy shield humming in the distance. I stare at Tula as the big cat stirs and crawls off me, shaking red flakes of failed combustion potion out of her fur.

The room's in ruins. Everything around me is pitch black and blood red from spell fall-out. The energy shield had been too late, but Tula wasn't. I sit up, unharmed and relatively intact. A scratchy, wet tongue licks my face, then I taste fur as Tula nuzzles my cheek.

"Seeing as you are the reason we almost blew up, I don't know if I can truly thank you for the save. But does this mean we're friends, now?" I scratch behind her ears, grimacing at the thick goo matting her fur.

She licks me again and pushes me down with a massive paw, standing on my chest. Onyx eyes stare into my soul, before she barrels through the door, taking advantage of her broken leash.

I stare at the black and red trail of footprints she leaves behind, hoping she's not going where I think she is. The sudden, strong smell of ice cutting through the stink of sulfur and burning wood tells me I was wrong to hope.

But *ayo*, I think she likes me.

I stay flat on my back for a moment longer, laughing.

THE BEDROOM:

My bed is not made for three. At least not
when the third person is a giant riorfox that
has dreams about running across plains. I'm
buried under mounds of fur, Tula draped
over my torso and legs, snoring, and Mehki
sleeping on my face. The little macram hates
Tula. He hides in closets, boxes, and keeps
to high shelves when she's in the house.

I reach up, grabbing him by his bushy tail
and peeling him off. He can sleep next to my
head if he's got to be on the pillow. It's too
hot for two furry beasts to be on top of me. I
narrow my eyes at Mehki, as he wakes up,
turning his foxy-face in my direction. His
glinting yellow gaze meets mine and he
shows me his sharp little teeth.

I run my hand along his rigid spine,
feeling how taut his muscles are. His tawny
fur prickles. "She won't be here forever,
buddy. The bed will be all yours again,
soon."

I usually don't let the shelter animals in
my bedroom. Mehki's never had to share. He
thinks his status as my only pet is being
challenged. He bit me twice this week and

refused to eat a few times too. He doesn't realize that Tula can't stay.

I grunt as he smacks me in the face with his tail and bullies my head off the pillow. I sit up, causing Tula to fall off my chest. Her head lolls backward, the rest of her body following and doing an impressive back flip off the bed. She growls deep, springing to her feet and spinning around in circles, looking for who did it.

Mehki chitters—his version of laughter, looking over the side of the bed, then sprawling out on his back over my *fipping* pillow. He gives me a foxy-smile and shuts his eyes. I stare, then grunt again as a heavy riorfox leaps back onto the bed, the brunt of her weight landing on my legs. She curls up and turns, butt in my face.

And I've had enough. Not caring if she falls again, I pull myself out from under Tula. Standing, I dump Mehki off my pillow, claiming it in the name of sleep, and stomp over to the corner where my saucer-lounger sits nestled between a desk and a bookcase. I throw myself down on it, putting the pillow behind my head and curling up. Let the beasts have the bed, whatever. Hope they eat each other.

I start as a big head nestles itself in my lap and look down to see Tula staring up at me. She yawns, breath sweet and sour, and purrs.

"This is comfortable for you?" Though I've seen cats sleep in stranger positions. However, she left a soft bed to crouch at my feet.

Guess we *are* friends.

She closes her eyes as I sink further into the cushion of my chair, stroking her behind the ears as I drift away.

~*~

VILITANDRA IS A DRY PLANET, twenty percent water, eighty percent land mass. Fifty percent of that land mass is desert, but the rest is flat grassy plains and forests with trees and plant-life that don't require much moisture. Prides of riorfoxes roam particular areas. A trade ship heading through the Cratperan System dropped us off on Vilitandra *cycles* ago and we shuttled to a wildlife center that gave us maps and patterns of several prides.

I sit in the spongy green grass, watching Tula and three other riorfoxes groom each other, using paws to sift through fur. An adolescent male riorfox rubs her cheek and she licks his nose. She was introduced to this pride fifty-six *jewels* ago and already they're family. As the obvious youngest, she's the lowest in the pecking order, having to eat last while the others feed. They let her sleep in the inner circle with the other young ones of the pride. The elders rest on the outskirts, keeping watch.

A hand touches my shoulder and a waft of earthy cinnamon brushes my nose.

"Having second thoughts?" Jalee smirks, but her large brown eyes are warm.

I frown in Tula's direction before looking back at my second-in-command. She sits

like a royal, back straight, hands folded in
her lap. Her long black hair is tied into a
plaited bun at the nape of her neck.

"Nah." My reply comes out easily, not a lie
then. "She's not pet material. Some
creatures aren't meant to be limited."

"Limited?" She raises a thin, straight
brow.

"Restrained, leashed, potential never fully
explored" I look beyond the pride, at the
black trees in the distance. "I couldn't do
that to her. And there's also the fact that
Adonis would put us both out."

Jalee chuckles, her laugh light and airy.
I've always liked the sound of it. "I don't
think I've ever seen him show so much
emotion in one week."

"Only one emotion though." I snort,
attention going to the full satchel resting in
the grass beside one of Jalee's knees. "Did
you find all the basa root you needed?"

"Yes." She caresses the raw-hide flap of
her bag. "There's nothing like getting to pick
it fresh. The imported stuff's so stale."

It's my turn to raise a brow at her and she

31

laughs again. "Just so I'm sure you know, I didn't come here with you just to pick roots. I came to make sure you'd be all right leaving your friend behind."

I grin. There was never a doubt in mind about why Jalee had accompanied me. The basa root just sweetened the deal for her. I'm glad she found some. I gaze back at Tula and her pride, watching them play. Two of the big cats study me. The pride got used to me hanging around after a *cycle* or so, but they're still wary.

I stand up, dusting off my cargos and holding a hand down to Jalee. My job here is done. "Let's head back to camp and signal for transport."

"Oh?" Jalee takes my hand. She tilts her head. "You're ready to go?"

I nod. "Yeah. She's found a family. They seem stable and content. What more can I do for her?" I shrug and turn, heading back in the direction of the night-camp Jalee and I had set up when we first arrived on the pride's grounds. It's about thirty *ka* away, a decent walk, far enough that Tula won't be able to smell me on the breeze anymore.

Jalee starts to follow and stops. "Ev."

I halt too, and throw a look over my shoulder as Tula comes to us. I smile, dropping to one knee to give her a final ear scratch and kiss between the eyes. "My friend, it's time for you to stay."

The command she never understood, because she's not to be commanded. She's free, in a way I'll never be. I rise to my feet, waiting a moment as the riorfox lays in the grass, eyes on me. "Stay."

I back away, a sense of loss and accomplishment overcoming me for a *wisp*, as Tula remains in place. After a few more steps, I turn around. Jalee joins me as we walk away, leaving Tula with her new family.

Jalee slings an arm over my shoulder. "One day, you'll get your chance at something like this too."

I frown at her, and she pulls me closer, into more of a one-armed hug. "You won't be leader forever. You'll get to retire and then, you can go where you want and won't have to listen to any councils telling you what to do."

When I'm old. And tired. And boring.

Jalee must sense my melancholy, because she squeezes my shoulder. "*Plikker* up, *mikob*! *Ayo*, when we get back home, I'll buy you a sweet ice with extra joca nuts."

"The kind that makes me hyper?" I ask with a smile.

"Hyper and crazy," she confirms. "And then, I'll let you spend the night at my flat so Adonis won't kill you."

I laugh, putting my arm over her shoulder. "I love it when you spoil me."
"I'm taming you, one treat at a time," she says. "And then, when you're old and free of us all, you won't forget where home is and will come back to us every once in a while."

"What makes you think I wouldn't take you all with me?"

We walk in companionable silence for a few *ka*, before I chance one last look over my shoulder. In the far distance, I see my riorfox, still laying in the grass where I'd left her. That brief sense of accomplishment returns for another *wisp* and I smile.

END

DAILY
DEVOTION

———∽∽∽———

Jalee Orcharest

A *CYCLE* BEFORE THE SUN comes up, I rise. Every morning, no matter the venue or how tired I am, my routine continues. I tiptoe through the dark room, careful not to step on my sleeping companions, and almost trip over a braided rope of dark golden hair. I can't resist touching it, picking the heavy braid up to drape over my dearest friend's back. It rises and falls with his breath as he sleeps deeply. Working fire and wind magic on a planet lacking a magical core is draining and the brunt of the spell had fallen on Evan.

36

Adonis had practically carried him back to our temporary bungalow.

He looks innocent when he sleeps, and much younger than the rest of us. Maybe it's the human in him, or the Magic Breed. Ember Sprites are eternally young, and it's not uncommon for their mixed descendants to stop physically aging during or after adolescence. Next year, Adonis, Desiri and I may all turn seventeen without Evan.

My feet are light across the soft wood floor. I hate that the bungalow only has one room. It makes privacy impossible, but it's cozy sleeping on floor pallets, listening to the gentle night-breathing of my court around me. No snoring, no panting, no tossing and turning. I'm comforted to know that all my friends are resting peacefully after a rescue mission that ended up being a body retrieval. We arrived too late to help, but the families of the fallen men and women had at least thanked us for giving them the means for blessed burials.

The season was the problem. Summers in this region are dry, so building death pyres for so many was not an option, and, here, ground burials are obscene. Without the money to pay for the bodies to be properly released in deep space, the Teroki people would have had to store their dead in cold boxes until Fall. We worked our magic for them, so that the pyres could burn, with the wind keeping the large flames contained and scattering the ashes.

Opening the front door of the bungalow, I smell the faint hint of sweet smoke still in the air. The villages nearby will reek of burial smoke for weeks yet. I step out onto cracked earth, noting a few tufts of dry yellow grass breaking through its surface. The bungalow is surrounded by dying woods. The trees are withered, leaves shrunken, but I'm told that in the Fall, when the rains come, this place rejuvenates. It must be beautiful, or why else would the Teroki stay in this area instead of joining the Meroka tribes on the greener plains?

Setting my rawhide satchel on the ground, I pull out a container of blessed water, a candle, a pouch of hani petals and a handful of orange carnelians cut like rounded fingernails. I sip the water, while using one hand to plant the candle in the dirt, circle it with gems, and fill the circle with petals. Once done, I tuck the water back into my satchel and dig a fuser out of the side pocket of my cargos. As I kneel and reach for the candle, the wick lights on its own.

Smiling, I turn my head to see Evan coming toward me, arms stretched over his head as he yawns.

"Did I wake you up?" I ask.

"The door did," Evan says, scrubbing a hand through his messy hair. Curls spring free of their braid and frame his soft features: wide green eyes fringed with thick, dark lashes, semi-full lips and a dimple that keeps him on my good side when he grins. Lots of people describe him as pretty, and even more people underestimate him for it. He takes special pleasure in knocking those types down in sparring sessions. A little guy with a lot to prove.

Though, as he continues to stretch, his tunic raising to reveal lean abdominal muscles, he's not so little anymore. We've known each other for seven *revs*—from children to adolescents. He stops beside me, dusky bronze skin touched by candlelight, and frowns.

"What?"

"Just looking at you," I say. "Did I wake everyone up?"

He grumbles under his breath, then asks, "What do you think?"

We know each other's movements so well that we can sleep through them, but no trained soldier should sleep through doors and windows opening and shutting unless they're drugged.

"I think it's weird that you didn't go back to sleep after you realized it was only me," I say. He hums and echoes my movements as I sit down in front of my ring of carnelians and press my palms together.

I gaze at him again. "You're going to do devotions with me?"

"It's interesting." He brings his hands together, mimicking me. "Kind of relaxing."

"You remember how?"

40

He grins, dimple flashing. "Not really. Show me again?"

Rolling my eyes and laughing lightly, I reach for my satchel and pass him the container of water inside. "Very well, student-mine. Have a drink and do as I do."

When we were kids, he liked for me to play teacher. I tutored him in potion-making and the art of lacing words with magic. He was an attentive student, inquisitive, bright. He never laughed at my traditions or beliefs. Remasians may praise Order, but they don't believe in Her. Their goddess is an ideal, an image to paint on buildings and carve into metal to represent their political prowess.

My goddesses are a way of life—were a way of life, before I came to Rema and had to change.

"Look into the candle flame, and breathe, slowly. In and out," I say softly.

Though magic-users can borrow strength from elements and living beings, the power to be able to do so comes from within. Dane and Niobe wrote in Their Book that our

41

cores need to be cleansed and reset at the start of each new *cycle*.

"Visualize your center." Everyone's core magic represents itself differently. Mine manifests as a flower that blooms when it's healthy, furls when it's injured and closes when it's recharging. The pale pink flower in my chest is closed, still gathering energy. My powers are at their strongest midday. It's a definite flaw, but one easily masked by skill. I'm better at imbuing objects with power and casting curses than anyone in my court.

I take deep breaths, staring at the candle flame and stroking my core with mental fingers. My magic is cool and smooth. I let its calm run through my limbs as I clear my mind of current tasks and leave it open to any random memories of moments and past impressions that want to wander through. Brief, disjointed threads of events, people and places flicker behind my eyes, as I fall under their spell.

~*~

A DECADE EARLIER

I kneel in front of the altar of Dane. My mother, beautiful with deep mahogany skin and onyx hair coiled in one thick braid around her head, gazes down at me. Her voice is sweet and kind as she tells me I am no longer part of the Danecian line of priestesses and that I'm to be sent away. She assures me it's not a punishment but a high honor, but I feel as if I've failed both her and the goddesses. Hot tears run down my cheeks.

~*~

MY HAIR IS OUT OF its braid and free to fall over my shoulders and down my back. Only priestesses and trainees can wear single braids, though my mother hadn't made me take it down until we arrived on Rema and

I was formally presented to the Remasian Council. My legs shake as a tall man with bright blue eyes and a woman with a pointy face, Councilors Theorne and Viveen, analyze me like something they've just purchased.

Mother's kind voice is curt in a way I've never heard before. "I will be remaining with my daughter, until I feel she no longer requires my presence. This is to be our understanding, or we will be leaving."

Council Theorne's voice is oily as he makes promises and compliments me, all the while Viveen scowls and glances at her timekeeper.

~*~

THE ATRIUM IS FULL OF tall trees and walkways made of glass. Someone is laughing—someone young—as if the funniest joke in the world was told, and I hate the sound. Nothing is funny when my life as I know it is ending. A boy with dark bronze skin and wild curly hair cartwheels

44

into my path, nearly knocking me over. His green eyes sparkle as he topples onto his back, laughing up at the glass ceiling offering a view of a bright purple Remasian sky.

"Are you the priestess?" he asks. His voice is higher than mine, and musical, like he's singing. He rolls onto his stomach, propping his chin in his hands and staring at me. "I'm Evan Lauduethe."

The future leader of Rema, the person I was brought here for, is a boy who rolls around on the ground. Another boy emerges from the trees, tall and brown-skinned with the opaque irises of a nymph. He watches me as he moves to Evan Lauduethe and grabs him under the arms, pulling him to his feet.

Evan smiles at me, a dimple appearing in one cheek. "Thank you for coming here. We'll do our best to get you used to everything. It, uh, must be hard to be here." He scratches the back of his neck. "All of us want to be somewhere else. But we can have fun here too. Right, Desiri?"

A girl steps onto the path, long coppery hair in double braids. Her yellowish eyes narrow and I notice the dragon-like shape of the barrettes in her hair. Poisoned pins.

I fight to keep a sneer off my face. A mage.

"*Ayo*, Priestess. Nice to meet you."

Both Evan and the nymph glance at the mage warily, the nymph probably sensing the mage's untruth. Evan clears his throat and the mage's hostile look lightens, as she turns it on him. She comes to stand beside Evan, and the nymph. The nymph is the tallest, Evan the shortest. The mage rounds out the middle.

"Meet my court," Evan says. "Adonis Maeve—he's my cousin, and a little bit of nymph. Desiri Lilias—she's a mage-trainee, and...you're Jalee Orcharest—our adept witch."

I hate that he calls me a witch. I hate that I'm expected to work with a mage. But Evan's warm smile keeps me off-guard. He's sunshine, and Dane and Niobe teach us to love and praise the sun.

"An honor to meet you." I take the hand he extends and hold it in mine.

~*~

MY SHOULDERS SHAKE AS I sob. I sit in the hot dirt, uniform torn and discolored by grime...and blood. Someone else's blood. Disciples of Dane and Niobe do not take lives, because every being is a creation of a god. Years after being taken from the temple, a year after my mother went back to Faran, I still pray. I still run my rituals. I give blessings, as if I'm still a priestess to be—but I can't pretend anymore. Not with blood on my soul.

I knew the time would come. There are only so many battles you can fight, so many deflection-shields I can cast, before lasics and blades need to be drawn and wielded. I never strike to kill. I disarm, I dazzle and daze, but today, it would have been my blood spilled in the dirt.

"I wasn't fast enough."

I start, raising my head to see Evan standing over me. He kneels in front of me. "I wasn't there in time. I'm—I'm sorry, Lee-Lee."

47

I swallow hard, studying the large bruise darkening half his face and the bandages wrapped around his hands. His hair is pulled back in a knot at the nape of his neck. It's getting so long, longer than mine. I reach up, running my hand along the long braid that I'm no longer supposed to wear. I'm not a priestess, not even a pretend one anymore. I'm not to be loved or praised.

"I... It's not your fault," I rasp.

And it's not. I'm supposed to protect him, not the other way around. That's my duty. I'm his witch adept. I build shields, brew potions, cast curses and imbue weapons with power.

He touches my face with bandaged hands. "You weren't ready to do that yet."

"And you were ready, when you first killed?" I ask. He'd vomited all night after the first time, but that had been a year ago. Now, he no longer hesitates. Desiri and Adonis never hesitate. They turn their feelings on and off.

I can't do that. Evan can't do that, but he can look at things in a different light. What

48

he does, he does for the Remasian people. He likes to see purpose in our tasks. When people thank him, he smiles and can believe that we've helped someone. For him, helping one person justifies the loss of another.

He smiles at me, dimple showing. "No. I'll never be ready, but we saved a transport vehicle full of kids today. They were going to be slaves in the Tgeri Territory. Now, they're going home."

The children—young children, practically babies. They'd cried for mothers and fathers that they'll see again now. I picture them laughing and playing, free of fear. The person—the woman I'd run through with a long blade—had wanted to sell those babies. She'd helped to steal them from their homes.

Does helping truly justify killing?

Does it?

Evan continues to smile at me, and he is sunshine, to be loved and praised. I reach back, ripping out my hair-tie and using my fingers to dismantle my false priestess braid. Only one person here deserves to wear one.

I look around as my hair falls free down my

back. The sky is hazy with machine smoke, but the clouds tells me it will rain soon. Remasian soldiers round up prisoners, babies are taken to shelter. Adonis and Desiri check inventories. This is downtime, rest time.

"May I braid your hair?" I ask Evan.

He blinks at me, smile faltering. "Huh?"

"Sit." I pull him down the rest of the way when he doesn't move, and shift, so that I'm behind him. I unbind his hair, finger-combing tangles before I section the curls and begin to braid.

~*~

NOW

I clear my mind of all past images and thoughts, breathing deeply, as the flame of the candle becomes visible again. I whisper to my student, "Clear your mind."

The petals of my core tremor, slowly opening, ready to receive the light of the day. Clear and cool. Serene and silent. I lean forward and blow out the candle, then sit back on my heels.

"And that..." I tilt my head, eyes scanning for Evan. Where did he...?

I chuckle at seeing him curled on his side, eyes closed, breathing even and soft, as he sleeps again. I reach out, running a thumb over his cheek, then letting my fingers caress his braid—my priestess braid—that he redoes after every wash, because it's special to me.

He murmurs in his sleep, in a language I don't speak, but I'm used to hearing from him. He utters about some undoubtedly human thing—Cheetos—and smacks his lips. I clean up the circle, putting away my materials. And after I'm done, I sit, reflecting on the day to come, our journey home, what our next mission will be, and how I will continue to love and praise the sun.

It is my daily devotion.

FRACTIONS

END

THE ALMOST ASSASSIN

—⚬⚬—

Desiri Lilias

UPO'S.

The name of the store almost turns me away because it's a Tepshan surname. Tepshan smithing is almost as *pidgy* as Tepshan schools of magic. But I need raw silver, all craft shops carry it, and Upo's is nearby. I can't wait until we get off this *sludgerock*, backwater, border planet. I'm tired of eyeballing my food for worms and needing to boil everything I drink. I slap a tiny buzzle from my bicep before it can suck blood and push through the thick black curtain functioning as the front door for Upo's.

Pidgepit.

A blast of cold air hits me in the face, stinging my eyeballs as it overcompensates for the sticky, sweltering heat of evenings on planet Mujbo—or Mush-bore, as I call it. The entire planet's a swamp with ramshackle, clay and wood townships thrown up in the four inhabitable parts of its surface. If it wasn't for the Nihto ore sleeping beneath its swamp beds, the Silver Allegiance would leave this planet to finish rotting around its suns.

A chime rings overhead, and I look up at the low, wooden ceiling. A mobile of slender, triangular crystals clank together, stirred by a weak protection spell I could rip apart in my sleep.

"Coming!" A male's voice trills with light vibrato from the back of the store. There's another curtain drawn across the backwall. Probably another room. I'm surprised this musty shack has an add-on.

The pale, wooden walls of the store have a sanded finish with built-in shelves lined with jars of powders, crystals, liquids, and little burlap sacks tied with twine. Barrels of mealy looking crap sit in the center of the room and, in the back corners, are racks of second-hand spell tools. I trek across the wood floor, leaving boot-prints in a day's worth of dirt other visitors probably brought in. I run my hands along the shelves, feeling the cracked grooves of the words carved in them, staring at the supplies. Some of the stuff looks viable, some of it looks like the *pidge* crooks sell beginners that don't know better. Easy coin.

The back curtain parts in the middle and a skinny guy in a brown, hooded robe steps out. His blue eyes are on the ceiling as he stretches his hands toward it, mini-light shows flickering blue and white between his fingertips. "Blessed be, my sister w—Oh."

"No, no, go on." I grin, folding my arms over my chest. "Blessed be, your sister what? I want the full-on floor show, before I tell you I know that the majority of your wares are *fipping pidge* and I only want to see the silver. If you got it."

The shop-keeper stares at me, a bit of fear flitting across his unlined, tan face, before the customer service smile returns. He drops his hands, minor magic dissipated, and lets his hood fall back. Short, white curls fall over his forehead, the kind of white that comes from sun-bleaching. He's not bad looking, the eyes are little far apart, nose a little bent, but I wouldn't be opposed to getting out of here with him a little later and finding some fun. Though fun and Mush-bore aren't exactly synonymous. He'd probably take me to his favorite fishing hole.

"Uh..." He scans my uniform, gaze lingering on the snake dagger on my utility belt. It's the only weapon I let be visible. My warning.

"You're with Leader Lauduethe. You're the mage, Honorable Lilias."

"What gives it away? The uniform, the knife?"

"The poison barrettes."

I touch an index finger to one of the dragon-eye barrettes clipping my bangs behind my ears. "You're observant."

"That's necessary in this business." The shopkeeper gives a tight bow at the waist. "I have silver in the back. Please, follow me." His back is straight as he re-parts his curtain and passes through.

I catch the edge of the fabric before it swings shut and step through. And stop short.

This...is a different store.

Like walking into another dimension, the atmosphere changes from cheap shack with bugs in the walls to a fancy, stone cellar with jewel-tone pillows on pedestals balancing sharps. Swords, daggers, short knives, medium and small bladed-discs. The aroma of leather and polished metal is my favorite cologne. I inch toward an obsidian stiletto dagger, a small ruby in its leather-bound hilt glints. I reach for it, palming the grip, fingers settling around it like it was made for my hand. It warms as it attunes to my magic, molding itself to suit my style.

I hear his step, sense his presence as he nears. My free hand shoots out, grabbing him by the throat of his robe and dragging him close. My boots make me taller than him by an *iut*. He chokes and struggles against my hold as his eyes bug out.

Fip. Can't have him passing out on me yet. I loosen my grip. Rolling my eyes as he sucks in a loud, exaggerated breath. Oh please. He didn't go *that* long without air. *Danderpris.* I give him a little shake, then let go.

He staggers back, rubbing his neck. Not daring to look away from me.

Not stupid then. "Where'd you get this dagger?" I spin the stiletto in my other hand.

He blinks, mouth flapping open like one of those ugly ass fat-lipped fish our Mush-bore hosts keep trying to feed us for breakfast, lunch, and dinner. A rush of irritation and flare of anger make me advance on him, slowly. A predator's stalk. One that tells him he's dead if he answers wrong. Or just doesn't answer.

I bring the blade up. Stilettos are for stabbing. An assassin's perfect weapon. "Why do you have a Viper's dagger?"

"I bought it!" The man backtracks into another pedestal. A blue pillow and several small bladed-discs clatter to the asphalt floor. "I didn't kill anyone if that's what you're thinking!"

I pause at that, and snort. Anger and irritation vaporize in a cloud of hilarity as I size up the scrawny shopkeeper. His fear smells like urine. Or perhaps that's just what's running down his legs right now as he trembles.

No, this man couldn't kill anyone. The thought of him challenging a Viper—laughter pokes my ribs like a tickle stick until I chuckle. The shopkeeper stares at me, and, for a *wisp*, I don't know if he's going to make a holy sign, run or scream for help. Though, I don't know who'd come. Mush-bore doesn't have law enforcement. It's kill or be eaten around here.

"So... are you...going to kill me?" His voice is small but doesn't shake like the rest of him. And suddenly, this is boring.

Of course he didn't kill a Viper, and he'd be dead if he stole from one. Which means, he's telling the truth. He bought it or found it, but from who or where? Answers to those questions are better taken from friendlier conversation. I slip the stiletto into my boot.

"I'll buy it off you, but you have to tell me who you bought it from. And I still want my silver." I wait. Give him a little while to let the fact that I'm not going to kill or even rob him sink in and let him shake off his terror.

Judging from his weapon store house all dolled up with pedestals and pillows, and fully stocked with decent sharps, this man gets a lot of fighting types back here. I watch him shrug his robe off and toss it behind him. A breeze of light magic catches the shed clothing and carries it to a counter in back.

The shopkeeper isn't bad at all. That bulky robe hid a slim muscled frame. In a brown sleeveless tunic and form fitting, dark denim pants, the man looks good. Like he could win a fight or two with people who aren't me. A small energy rifle is clipped to a belt around his waist.

I glance at his face, pleased to find the 'scared act' all gone. And, hah. It hadn't been piss I smelled earlier. "Your rifle's powered by Nihto ore." That *pidge* reeks.

I narrow my eyes, reassessing. I thought he couldn't kill anyone. I've been wrong plenty of times before, but not this wrong. This guy could kill, but—

I move. I'm at his throat. Snake blade at his jugular before he can react.

—he couldn't kill a Viper.

He gasps but doesn't struggle. Smart people don't when sharps are against their necks.

"Okay." I retract my snake blade, and casually pluck the rifle off his belt. Doubt he felt it. I'm a good thief. Distract them and take what you need before they recover.

He turns as I step back, eyes widening at his weapon in my hand. I click it into safety mode and toss it back. A show of good faith. Killing customers that offer to pay is bad business and judging from the fact that he hasn't made a single defensive move, he's not going to try it.

He's going to make a sale instead.

That customer service smile from earlier slides back in place and he earns another chuckle from me. But this one's from a different place. I think I'm going to ask him out after this.

"That was some good acting," I say. "What's your name?"

"Wique." He clips the rifle back onto his belt. "You didn't believe it."

"I did for a bit." I shrug. "Thought you'd peed yourself. You deserve a drink after all this."

His smile widens, then he nods down at my boot, where I'd slipped the stiletto. "I'll buy myself a fancy one after you pay me for that. It's expensive."

"You said you bought it?"

"Off a mage."

"What guild?" I run through the names of strong mage guilds that would go after a Viper Assassin and could win.

"Viper. A legacy. Just like you were supposed to be."

I put away my snake blade, careful not to visibly react while my brain shouts *vati fipping pidge*. A legacy Viper selling a Viper's stiletto in the backwoods. Treason, murder, and nothing I want any part of has me backing

63

toward the curtain that let me in. I retrieve the weapon from my boot, ready to lay it back on its pillow on my way out.

"The mage who sold it to me was Dalton Lilias."

Dalton.

I halt in my tracks as my blood boils hotter than the swamp water cooking under Mushbore's soon to go nova sun.

Do. Not. Visually. React.

Instead, I hold the dagger in my grip, letting it meld with my magic again. It feels so right in my hand. Like it's mine. And now I know why. It's a legacy blade, crafted specifically for mages from one of Viper's seven founding families.

I turn back to Wique, expecting to find him awaiting my response and am not disappointed. He knows he's got his sale. But first, I need to know.

"Why was my brother here?"

~*~

A DECADE EARLIER

I VISUALIZE THE SUMMONING SPELL for fire, its runes flashing through my mind as I charge them with magic. A spark ignites on the conjuring plane—a pocket dimension for spellworkers. I channel the fire into my palms. The pommels of my daggers blaze as I hurl controlled flames at my brother in short bursts.

He cuts each fire blast with his own conjured flames and channels spirals of ice-wind at me through his daggers. I cross mine, catching the wind where the blades meet and pushing out. The wind howls as it goes wild, blowing Dalton off his feet. He turns his fall into a backflip and goes down in a crouch.

I drop into a lower stance, one knee forward, ready. I don't know if Dalton's going to spring up and rush me or blast me with a spell. He's as good as I am at visualizing, so he doesn't need to say magic words. The easiest people to crush are magic users who have to speak or mouth incantations. The dummies tell me what they're doing before they do it. I counter-cast faster than most people my age. The only kid who keeps up is Dalton. But he's a *critch-cratch*, so I can't tell him he's good.

Black smoke ripples from Dalton's red bodysuit.

I throw up a quick and dirty protective barrier.

Black smoke. Wavy pattern. What spell is it? It's not Shadow Grab. Is it Black Mirror? No. I'd see my reflection in the smoke.

I reach for the pouch of *ether* dust hooked on my belt—and jump back as a shadow clone punches at my face.

I need light! The rune flares in my head and I charge and channel it. My vision goes white as a wall of brightness flattens Dalton's stupid clones.

Gili mas! Dalton can do Shadow Puppet. Since when?

Dark clouds snuff my light. A transparent Shadow Clone wriggles out of the darkness

66

and staggers toward me. It's weak as *pris,* body fading with each step. I rip it apart with a wind hail and wait, daggers up.

The storm cloud starts to vaporize, and I grin. I knew *critch-cratch* couldn't hold that. I ready more fire, letting it dangle from my blades like red hot ropes.

Whatcha' gonna do, big brother?

I see his feet before the rest of him. He's coming, but... was that a wobble? Did *critch-cratch* put too much power into that last move? I snap a fire rope at his left foot. He dodges, almost too slow.

The cloud is completely gone. Dalton's exposed and—*critch-cratch* flies at me. I duck a roundhouse and come up in an uppercut that grazes his jaw. His spin-kick catches my ankle. I fall into a front handspring kick-out that kisses air. Bouncing back on my feet, I square up, glaring into Dalton's amber stare. We've got the same eyes, but his are meaner, I think.

Dagger fight. Our blades go strike for parry.

Cling-clang. Cling-clang.

I visualize the wind hail runes and pull the power through my arms. Releasing and letting the storm go wild because I can't direct the gale winds. My hands are busy. Something cracks and groans to the left. Sounds like a—

"Stop."

A tree crashes to the ground between us. Dirt flies. I turn my head to avoid it getting in my eyes. Across from me, Dalton sneezes.

"What have I told you about untamed magic?" Fasa's voice is like cold rain, always. No matter what he says or feels, my father sounds the same.

But—I toe the fallen red tree with my boot. He loves these red trees. Brought them over from his home planet, Kaya, before I was born. So, he's probably mad. I cringe and bow my head. "Untamed magic is a show of weakness because it signifies a lack of skill and refinement." I don't imitate his accent. Last time I did that, I ended up polishing all of Fasa's knives.

He's got a lot of knives. I lost count after one-hundred and sixty-seven.

I tuck my daggers in my belt and turn, hands flat against my sides, standing at attention as Fasa inspects me. He's a mountain, wide shoulders, and big upper body. He's skinnier on bottom. Mim calls it 'tapered' and licks her lips when Fasa struts by in his black and gray bodysuits.

"Decent summoning. Excellent conjuring speed. Graceful footwork."

"Thank you, Fasa." My ears burn as I squeeze my lips together to keep from smiling. Fasa never sugars his critiques. If a person's trash, they're trash, even if it's me or Dalton. Both Fasa and Mim believe everyone needs the truth when it comes to fighting. Mistakes cost mages their reputation. A bad rep means no jobs. No jobs mean no coin.

"Dalton." Fasa moves on, going to stand in front of my brother. Dalton raises his chin. "Decent firebreaks. Sloppy footwork. Inadequate combat strategy as you did not account for early fatigue due to over-training before a sparring session. You've been spoken to about this."

"Yes, Fasa. Sorry, sir."

"Apologies are worthless."

Dalton doesn't flinch as Fasa's amber eyes wear him down. I steel my spine to keep from shivering, glad Fasa's doomsday glare isn't on me. I never get the doomsday daggers. I usually get a few excellents and minor corrections. Dalton's the one who gets scolded for doing things he's not ready for. Fasa hates that worse than uncontrolled magic. A loss of control is an accident. Mages unleashing something they're not ready for is stupid.

"Desiri."

I start, tearing my attention from Fasa and Dalton to see Mim enter the yard.

"It's time." Mim walks across our warded practice field, avoiding craters blown into the ground from explosions and fallen branches the trees Dalton and I ruined. Our backyard is a miniature battlefield, all black dirt and white-chalked spell circles for casting. Fasa's red trees form a boundary line around us meant to separate our yard from the small forest our house hides in.

"Already?" Fasa places a hand on Dalton's

shoulder but looks to Mim. "I thought we had four more *jewels*. It will only take two *jewels* for you to reach the Hall of Decision."

The Hall of Decision. I frown, remembering Mim mentioning something about that at dinner a few nights ago. There'd been honey cake and I got to eat Dalton's because he was on punishment for breaking one of his lances during training. I licked honey off my fingers while Mim and Fasa talked. They'd said my name a few times, but...

"That's today?" I ask.

"Yes, *babila*," Mim says. "You are being tested today, and I would like to present a clean child in clothes that don't smell like a firepit."

"Tested?"

"Yes," Mim says. "Come."

Fasa nods for me to leave, and squeezes Dalton's shoulder. "Re-take your resting stance."

Envy pinches my underarms as I watch Dalton fall into a natural stance with his blades. I want to fight him some more. Stay

71

out here with Fasa and learn something new.
But...

"Desiri. I won't tell you to come again."

I bite down on a groan as I follow Mim to
the backdoor of the house. I want to drag my
feet. The Hall of Decision is a boring place
in the First Dome where the leaders and the
councilors live. They wear stiff uniforms and
practice synchronized combat in groups.
They use energy weapons instead of magic,
because most Remasians don't have magic.
I don't want to have a chance at being part
of a loser army. Even if it'd be a special job
with the leader apparent. Because that's what
Mim and Fasa had said while I kicked Dalton
under the table for trying to swipe a piece of
cake off my plate.

I enter the house. It's warm, the same
temperature inside as it is outside. A mage
should be able to make-do in all settings. The
main room is big and mostly empty. A low,
wooden meal table sits knee-high in the
center of the floor. Scrubbed clean from our
breakfast crumbs, our seat pillows freshly
dusted and pushed beneath the table. The

kitchen is dark with no smell of cooking food. Meaning lunch and dinner will probably be cold meals. Meat wraps and fruit. Light, cold meals usually tell me that we're going to run night drills.

I love night drills through the forest, playing hunter and getting to use my throwing knives. Mim and Fasa hide, and Dalton and I search the for them. We've never found them, but every time we go out, we get better. One day, my covered throwing knife is going to bounce off Fasa's head.

"We don't have time to wash your hair, but you can bathe. And you'll wear your whites."

Not the whites. The whites are long pants and sleeves with a stiff color and too many buttons. But I nod. "Yes, ma'am."

I follow her to the bathing chamber. The sunken tub is already filled with blue-pink water that smells like ripe yi-gi fruit. I strip out of my dirty practice clothes, then lower myself into the lukewarm water.

I hate baths. I prefer showering in the stalls outside near the practice field. It's faster and I don't smell like fruit or flowers after. Dalton never has to smell sweet. Mim sits on the edge of the tub, rolling up her long pants and setting her legs in the water. She gestures for me to place myself between them, meaning she's going to wash me. She never trusts me to get all the grit out of my nails.

She secures my hair on top of my head with pins and gets to work rubbing down my skin with a brush and pinkish foam lather. She hums as she works, a sad, slow song that had words a long time ago, but Mim says her grandmother forgot them before she could teach anyone.

I relax as Mim works. Though I really hate sitting in dirty water, I like spending alone time with Mim. Sharing her with Dalton is the pits. And if I'm not sharing her with him, then it's with Fasa, or she's on a job. She said she was going to start taking me with her soon, so I could meet more of the guild. Study them, learn habits and form bonds, because in a few *revs* I'll be an apprentice. An almost Viper.

"Mim?" I chance talking. Sometimes, it's not good to speak before being spoken to, but when it's just us—just me and her—it's different. I feel like I can a break a few rules, and Mim will smile and wink, like she doesn't do for Dalton. I'm sure she doesn't. I'm her special one. Dalton's ten Common-Years old, a full *rev* older than me. He should get first pick on what guild to join, Mim's or Fasa's. Mim's is the best. He wants to be with the Vipers, but Mim's going to choose me. I feel it.

"Mimmy?" I try again.

"Yes, *daja-mir?*"—my beautiful daughter.

"Why are we going to the House of Decision? I'm not going to join the army. I'm going to be one of your Vipers."

Because Mim's from one of the seven founding noble houses, she's a lord. She has her pick of the best jobs and selects who goes. I'm going to be one of her Hands or Eyes, and a future house lord.

"Because," Mim takes one of my hands and scrubs under my short nails, "the leader apparent of Rema is just about your age and is a strong magic user."

"A...? But he's, like, half-human and you

said his dad's a *goot*." Mim hates Devrik Lauduethe, calls him this weird word—'wanton'—and useless. A trash heap of wasted genes.

"It seems that all that magical blood that flows inactive in him, awakened in his child." Mim finishes my left hand and picks up my right. The bristles of the brush tickle, then burn as she goes after the dirt. "The Council is assembling a magical court for him, and they are sending them off-planet for magical defensive and offensive training." The brush pauses. "Do you know what that means, *daja*?"

Off-planet. They'd leave here and learn magic skills from other people—maybe even powerful people.

"*Mages only respect power.*" A memory of Fasa's voice is clear in my head.

"The leader and his court are going to be powerful," I say.

Mim hums and raises the hand she's been brushing, kissing my knuckles and letting my hand go. "You will be powerful. Think of the plethora of training you'd have access to. The novel techniques. The contacts you'll make."

"And bring them to Viper? Because can I be a Viper too?"

"We already have Vipers in the family. We do not have a career mage who will be on the foreground when this planet makes powerplays to be one of the controlling bodies in the joint Allegiances. This ambitious little world was a fine choice afterward." Her voice goes distant on the last sentence.

Mim and Fasa are from the same home world. A place of full jungles, wild magic, and warring mage guilds. They left when their guilds wouldn't approve their marriage. They settled here, on Rema, in the Third Dome. The one not gunked up with tech and tall buildings, the wildlife reserve. Mim and Fasa set up base and took rogue jobs until the Vipers and Fasa's guild, Tirge, accepted their vows. But they stayed and worked from here instead of going back.

Lessens the chance of knives in the back, they said.

But it meant only having one training partner my age for me. Though he's a *critch-cratch*, when Mim and Fasa take us to Kaya for guild competitions, he wins as much as I do. We get put in matches with the bigger kids and whip their butts. Everybody talks about it.

Which is probably why... "Mim, why did that council pick me to come? Why not Dalton? The kid leader's a boy, right? Don't they usually want other boys on their teams?"

Though only a *fromp* would want Dalton over me.

"The little leader has a strong affinity for fire, *daja*. Flame is your element of choice. Dalton is going to choose air. Plus," Mim pats my head "you're more likeable than *daj mir*"—my beautiful son. Who has the personality of a mud troll.

I snicker, but my stomach feels funny. Heavy, like my arms and legs all of a sudden. "If I end up getting picked to go with the leader, then—"

"You'll go to the First Dome. You'll have a dormitory with top tier amenities."

Mim doesn't sound sad. Won't she miss me?

"Mim?"

"No other family in Viper or your Fasa's Tirge will have the honor we do. You'll be a warrior mage who is not a rogue or contracted mercenary."

She sounds as happy as she did when she got word that one of my older sisters, who I never met, married into royal mage guild on Syih-ti. She never talks about her other kids with another Viper mage, two adult sisters that abandoned Viper to run with other guilds. Fasa doesn't talk about his other kids either, all adults. They don't accept Mim.

"Stand," Mim says.

I get up, knee-deep in murky water and turn to watch Mim getting a large white towel from a cabinet. The bath chamber is plain, with brown stone walls and floors, and cabinets carved into the stone. It traps heat, and doubles as a sweat room. Mim brings back the towel, shaking it out as she moves.

She's so pretty, dark-skinned, and dark-eyed, with thick black hair in springy ringlets shaped to frame her narrow face. I don't look like her at all. Fasa's burnt sand colored skin and amber eyes got passed to me and Dalton. Her other daughters look like her. Sometimes, I wonder if she ever loved them more than me because people looked at them and knew they were hers.

Mim wraps the towel around my shoulders. "Dry off, *daja*, and braid your hair. A big braid down the middle and a small one on either side. No beads, no lose hair. I'll bring in your clothes. We'll leave when you're dressed."

I rub myself dry, then tie the towel like a short dress around my body and go to my small room. A single bed tucked in a corner, a tiny desk, a tall mirror, and a cabinet carved into a stone wall makes up my space in this house. If I go, will Mim and Fasa use this room for something else? When mages leave their family homes, all of their stuff goes with them, including their memories. It's like they never lived there. I don't want to be erased.

80

E. ARDELL

My chest aches, and for a wisp, I want to be a bad daughter. I want to fling myself on the bed and refuse to get ready. But...

That's not what I do. I sit at my desk and spin the tiny, cushioned chair around to face the mirror. I attack my curly, copper hair with a bone-tooth comb, parting it, oiling it, then braiding with swift, callused fingers. Mim brings in my dress clothes and watches as I shrug into them.

She smiles lightly, her lips are painted a dark plum and her eyes are lined with color. Mim only wears makeup to important gatherings and meetings. She even wears her dress blacks with golden bangles on her wrists and in her ears.

"Mim...?"

"This is a job, *daja mir*. Your first and perhaps only job."

I swallow. My first and only job, as a mage. Not many mages have first and only jobs. Those mages work for royals, not armies. "Mim, I'm..." I can't say I'm getting scared, or I don't like it, or don't want it, because Mim wants it for me.

81

Her dark eyes sparkle and she kisses the top of my head. "We'll eat in the First Dome."

Fasa and Dalton are in the main room when we leave mine. They sit around the meal table, legs crossed. Fasa gets up and comes to me, putting his hand on top of my head.

"Honor us today, *daja*. You have always brought me pride. I know that you will not disappoint me."

My fingers, toes and tips of my ears burn, and my cheeks hurt from the grin stretching them too far. Fasa said...

I want to hug him, but I don't. We don't do hugs. And kisses are received, not given. The pat on the head is Fasa's kiss.

"I hope you get it," Dalton says.

I look at him as I stand between both our parents. Fasa's hand is still on my head and Mim is smiling at me. Dalton is alone at the table.

"Uh...thanks?" Because Dalton never hopes for me. He hopes for himself. If I get it, I'll move away. And maybe all my head pats from Fasa and smiles from Mim will go to him.

Dalton seems to read my mind. He smirks and reaches for a roll of bio-skin on the table. One of his sleeves is rolled up and a strip of shiny, burned flesh stretches from wrist to elbow.

"Did I—" I start to ask, but Mim grabs my shoulder.

"Let's go, Desiri. Our tram leaves soon."

Fasa walks us to the door and watches as Mim and I load into Mim's sleek, black railer that we'll leave parked at the tram station. Mim drives, humming tunelessly, as I watch our home grow smaller through the back window.

I know I'll see it again, soon. But my body numbs at the thought that the next time I gaze at our shrinking house through this window might be the last.

~*~

THE HALL OF DECISION IS boring. It's all white walls and floors and old people. They wear gray tunics and slacks and use big words. Their eyes rove over me to linger on Mim. A lot of the people here think she's beautiful and they offer her drinks and snacks and places to rest. Mim has no use for any of it. She gets right to business, because that's who she is.

We walk down a hallway and a door to a playroom opens. There's a grassy field full of trees with ropes swings and rope ladders connecting branches of trees. Someone inside is laughing and shouting for someone else to count. The accent is weird.

"Wait in there," Mim says, pushing me through the playroom door. "I'll return in a little while."

My mouth opens, but I won't ask "huh?" in front of strangers. It'd embarrass Mim. Instead, I stay put as she walks away with four men and two women in gray outfits. They talk as Mim nods, heading on down the hall. The playroom door slides shut on its own.

There's no sound, but I feel someone coming. Nearness sets off mental alarms. I spin around, dropping into a crouch and kicking out. The person yelps—but my foot never makes contact. The boy jumps out of the way, and stumbles back a few steps before catching his balance.

"That was so cool!" He grins at me, and I stare. He comes up to my chin. His curly bronze hair makes him seem a little taller, but he's not. "Are you a mage? We met two yesterday and another the day before."

I study him. He's scrawny with big green eyes and long lashes like a doll's.

What...is this?

I can't help it. I go to poke him in the belly, and he catches my hand. The movement was so quick I'm not sure if I really saw it. But it happened. He has my hand. He lets go, when I glare at him.

"I'm Evan." He waits.

"Lauduethe?" I ask.

"Yeah." He sticks his hands in the pockets of his denims. His yellow tunic is tucked into the pants. "I'm...uh...the leader to be."

I nod, frowning. There's not much to this *igik*. I want him to pull off his shirt so I can see the Mark of Order on his back. Otherwise, maybe I don't believe him.

I don't hear anything again, but I sense someone else coming close. I snap my head to the left and see another boy practically materialize from one of the trees. This one's taller with black hair and gray eyes that don't blink.

A sharp wave of panic hits. I take a fighting stance.

I don't have any weapons. Mim made me leave them behind, but I can fight hand-to-hand. Only, I don't know if people actually fight nymphs and win. And I know I can't run, because they're fast and get really excited when they have to chase their food. Does the council know a nymph got in? Or that it's in here with their leader apparent?

"I think you're scaring her, Adonis," Evan says to the nymph.

The nymph stops coming toward us, tilting its head.

86

"Um... I think we should..." I start, but Evan laughs.

"That's my cousin, Adonis," he says. "He's on my inner court. Like you want to be."

"I don't want to be on your stupid court." My voice doesn't shake, but I keep my eyes on the nymph. It's not eating me today.

"Then why are you here?" Evan loses the smile, and I'm glad. I hate when strangers smile too much. It's fake.

"Because my mother wants me to be on your stupid court." I cross my arms over my chest.

Both Evan's brows raise. "You're really honest."

"Hey! Stop right there." I point at the nymph, because it's moving again.

"He's not going to bite you," Evan says. "I'm more likely to do that. What's wrong with you?"

"What's wrong with me? There's a Magic Breed loose in here and you're... Were you playing with it?"

Evan copies my pose, arms over his chest. "Stop calling him 'it'. His name is Adonis.

87

He is my cousin. And he is not a—okay, so maybe he's a little bit Magic Breed. But so am I. And we're fine. Mixed blood."

I put distance between me and him too. "You're a mixed Breed?" Has to a Quarter-Breed or an Eighth. He's too smart to be more than that. Fae may be all powerful, but they're really dense. Give them a riddle and they might get so distracted they forget to hunt you.

"Yeah," Evan says. "From a long, long, long time ago. Great-great-grandparents. Same for him." He nods to the nymph—Adonis, who is almost to Evan's side.

I feel my muscles relax before my brain finishes processing what he said. "So, you don't eat people or chase them till they die, or drown them or make them disappear?"

Evan looks puzzled. "No. Did you think we would do that?"

I shrug.

Adonis reaches Evan's side and looks me up and down without a word. His stare is bottomless. My skin crawls but I don't shudder. I'm a mage. We don't let strangers see fear or weakness. I messed up enough by jumping back and asking those questions.

I need to change the dynamic. Give myself some footing. "What are we supposed to do until the council and my mother come back?"

Evan's annoying grin returns. "Well, I heard that the mage coming today is good with fire. Are you good fire?"

I shrug again, not giving anything away. "I hear the leader apparent has an affinity for fire magic."

Without a magic word or a pause for summons, fire erupts in his cupped hands. "You heard right. Wanna play?"

Adrenaline pumps through my veins as excitement makes my muscles bounce. I wanted to keep fighting Dalton today, but that got cut short so I could meet this teeny-tiny future leader. The way I see it, he owes me a spar to make up for the training I'm losing today.

So, "Yeah, let's spar."

Adonis sighs and walks away, disappearing into the trees again. Is he

89

climbing them or what? I don't know. Maybe I don't care right now, because I feel the heat of Evan's fire as he separates it. Flames burn in both his palms.

"Show me your fire magic," he says.

"Will I get in trouble if you get burned?" I ask.

"I don't burn." His confident little smile makes me laugh.

Okay, *gak mopi*. I visualize the runes for fire and pull it into existence. Fire swirls around my head, the cyclone dropping until it touches round. I let it wind around my body, like a shield.

Evan's mouth is an 'o' of awe. "Let me try that." And his flames zig from his hands, circling his body and copying mine.

I reach into my fire cyclone, gripping flame and spooling it around my arms like ropes. Evan mimics my move again. Okay, leader. Let's see you copy this.

I whip one of my fire ropes at him and he catches it, like he did my hand earlier. He holds my fire and tugs. I jerk forward, flying off my feet and landing hard on my knees.

That was a *juking* hard pull. Nothing that small should be that strong.

I get up, trying to yank my fire rope back, but it's like tugging a stone wall. The little leader doesn't budge. Instead, he looks at me. The cocky grin is gone. His face is alight, his eyes dance. He's happy about something.

"You can fight with your fire," he says.

"Yeah." I tug my rope again. This time he moves forward, but I think it's because he wants to. "I'm a mage. We fight with everything."

"That's so cool." He douses his flame and mine.

What the—he put out my fire? I get my fists up.

"Whoa." He stops *iuts* away. "I'm not gonna attack you. I—I just..." He digs a toe into the grass. "I know how to use magic. How to call fire, earth, air...and water." He sneers when he says 'water'. "But I don't know how to fight with it. Not yet. I can defend and shield, but I only know how to attack with weapons and my body. There's nobody here to show me. Will you show me some moves?" Wide, clear green eyes are open and honest and...making me feel something.

This kid wants *me* to teach him something? Me? "I'm not even an apprentice mage yet. I'm training."

"So?"

He says it easily. Carelessly. And I like it.

I look around. The playroom's all trees and grass and rope toys. No adults, no animals. "No one's going to get mad if we char this place?"

Evan follows my gaze around the room and it's his turn to shrug. "Someone's always mad at me. Whatever. They can fix it back, they've got money. Show me something awesome and let me try it."

A wild feeling takes over. It's hot and electric, charging me with energy and a want to have fun and experiment with the boundaries of this place. "Okay. You asked for it!"

And I let him have it. I show him some of my fanciest conjures. Making fire dragons that wrap around trees but don't burn them.

I show him fire snakes and back them up with wind hails to make the fire plume across long distances.

He watches and repeats my moves, over and over and until he gets a couple right. They're weak and shaky imitations, but really good for a beginner. I offer critiques and stand back, feet apart, nodding my head—like Fasa, as Evan applies corrections.

"Decent"—for the fire snake he made that kept its form for more than a minute.

"Again"—for the headless fire dragon.

We work for nearly an hour. Until the leader finally drops to his knees, dark brown skin covered in a sheen of sweat. I sit beside him and get the urge to pat his head like Fasa would. Sharp grass pokes me though my clothes, and I ignore it.

The nymph, Adonis, drops from a nearby tree and comes to us. He stares at me as I tense, then relax. If he wanted to eat me, he'd have done it already. And besides, now that I really look at him, he's not so scary. He's just got creepy eyes...and doesn't talk or blink.

Adonis sits beside Evan, blank eyes still on me.

"Can you do that with water?"

I blink. His voice is lower than Evan's but just as musical. I bet he can sing. Bet they both can. But his question. "Ah... I'm not as good with water, but I know the basics."

He nods. "Next time, you'll show me."

"Okay." As if there'll be a next time. "You said other mages were here before me."

"Three," Evan says. "But I think you'll be back, and they won't."

Curiosity ticks inside me like a good, old-fashioned bomb. "What makes you say that?"

"Because I like you." Simple as that. "You're good at magic. You didn't try to kiss my butt and let me think I'm better than you. And you didn't actually run from Adonis."

"That was a test?" I snap, glaring at them both. Evan flashes a dimple. Adonis's face never changes. "You little *critch-cratch*!"

Evan rolls in the grass, laughing. "A booty-butt face?"

I scowl at him. "Yeah. A big one!"

He keeps laughing and I roll my eyes. I put my attention on the nymph—Adonis. "Is he always like that?"

Adonis's eyes rove over to his cousin, then back to me. A solemn nod.

Okay. "Do you only speak like once a day?"

A single eyebrow raise.

What do I do with someone who doesn't talk?

Evan sits up, covered in grass. "He talks more when he gets to know you. Keep talking at him. He'll give in."

"Was that your strategy?" I ask.

"Yup." He springs to his feet. "Do you want to climb with me? Swing on the ropes?"

Basically: Do I want to play kid games? Mages don't play games. Not without a training purpose. I could make one up. Use it to train myself and him too. I rub my chin, about to brainstorm, when—

"Desiri, it's time to go home."

The playroom door is open, and Mim stands in the portal. She doesn't look happy or disappointed. She gestures for me to come to her, and I get up, dusting grass off my clothes.

Before I can walk to her, Evan grabs my wrist.

"Hey, we'll play next time. Okay?" He smiles, and my lips quirk upward, reflecting his smile without my permission.

I didn't mean to smile at him, but I did, and I want to. Earlier he said he liked me. Maybe I like him too. A little bit. And I'd like to play a game.

Only, Mim doesn't look happy, and she said we were going home.

I wasn't tested, wasn't quizzed. Never met the real council.

My world crumbles. I keep my eyes low and don't look back as Mim and I walk down the hallway. A woman in gray escorts us out of the building. No one says anything. No one has to. Somehow, I'd failed the test I was brought to take without even taking it. I won't do the things Mim wanted me to do as part of the leader's court. I won't make Fasa proud today.

Tears burn in my eyes on the entire tram

96

ride between the Remasian Domes—three large biospheres, protecting the inhabitable parts of the planet from space attack. The ride takes a *jewel* but feels like forever.

I sniffle. Stupid nose keeps running. Mim passes me a handkerchief and looks out the window. Ignoring me. I bite my lip and sit up straighter than ever. I embarrassed Mim twice today. First, I flunk a test and now I'm a snotty little kid. I should have tried harder when I went into the Hall. Should have seemed more like I wanted to be there.

I goofed around with the leader. Maybe the Remasian Council had watched and saw that my fire hails were weaker than normal. That I hadn't put their scrawny leader apparent on his butt. That I let the nymph rattle me. That was the test I bet. I should have glared Adonis down and sent the leader sprawling when he wanted to see my fire. Dalton would have. Meaning Dalton would have passed.

I screwed up and Dalton and everyone else will know.

I ball up Mim's handkerchief and stuff it

in my pocket. I don't need it. I'm not crying. Never. I'll fight harder. I'll beat Dalton into the dirt, and he'll forget. I'll do it so good, that Fasa and Mim will forget too. Then, things will go back to normal.

I remember the light in the little leader's eyes when he asked me to teach him, when he wanted to play. Gloom feels like stone bricks sitting on my chest. It's harder to breathe, and I want it to go away.

So, I'll beat Dalton into the dirt so hard, and so good, that like he, Mim and Fasa, I'll forget too.

~*~

WE ENTER THE HOUSE TO eat a cold dinner. Dalton stares at me, Mim and Fasa talk to each other through glances. My food goes down like rocks and I spend most of dinner pushing greens and raw fish around my plate. I stare at spells and strategies on my compal screen during reflection hour, but don't read them. I can't concentrate. I screwed up big and can't show anyone that it's better this way until tomorrow morning when I spar with Dalton again.

I go to bed without a goodnight kiss and the tears come back. This time, they run down my face. I wipe them away with the heel of my hands each time one reaches my chin.

I'll fix this. I'll be the best Viper there ever was. No one, but Dalton would be disappointed then.

I fall asleep thinking of faster ways to summon fire...and water, because I'd told the nymph I'm not good at it. I'll focus on making water spires and washing Dalton away. He won't know what hit him. He'll expect fire.

His stunned, angry face is the one I should see right now, but instead, I fall asleep wondering what game the little leader would have wanted to play with me before I had to go.

I'll never know.

~*~

I LEARN A TECHNIQUE CALLED waterfall, and coat Dalton in ice water so many times he gets sick. Sparring with a sick Dalton is almost better than a healthy one. He's more aggressive to make up for his fuzzy movements, and I have to think faster on my feet. He doesn't follow any patterns, trying to end all of our matches before he's too dizzy to fight back properly.

"Stop."

Fasa's voice rings across the practice field. I pull back my water spears and turn to face him. Dalton's breath wheezes behind me. The hot wind drying out my cheeks and eyes dies out—meaning he's shutting down his next attack too.

"Desiri. Go inside." Fasa nods at me. "Excellent footwork. Decent waterfall."

100

I beam on the inside and bow slightly. As I walk past him, he pats my head, then tells Dalton, "You will spar with me. Your stamina is poor, and your movements are unfocused. Fever is not an excuse."

I open the backdoor, tempted to stick my tongue out at Dalton, and freeze at Fasa's next words to Dalton. "A Viper must always be at their best."

The oats I had this morning touch the back of my throat. 'A *Viper must be...*' to Dalton. To Dalton! But I'm the one who's going to Viper, not him.

Why did Fasa pat my head? I grip the doorframe. I screwed up again.

"*Daja mir*, come in, close the door."

Mim kneels at the meal table. She sounds calm, formal. Like when she has potential employers come for dinner. I slowly make my way to her, heart heavy. Eyes burning. I hate stupid tears.

"Sit."

I do as told, folding my hands in my lap. I keep my eyes down.

"Look at me, *daja*." Mim's voice softens as

101

I raise my head. Her dark eyes are warm, bright. "You will not be saddened at the fact that you're leaving us."

I start, surprise so sharp in my gut it hurts. "Leaving—?"

"We will start transferring your belongings to the First Dome at sunrise. The Remasian Council would like you settled by noonday, so that you can begin your first diplomacy lesson with the leader apparent and the other member of the court."

What? I touch my chin to make sure my mouth isn't hanging open. What is Mim saying? Lessons. My stuff is going to the First Dome? "I passed the test?"

Mim's smile is slow, but easy. The one I want, but my feelings are mixed. I want to be a Viper. To stay here. But me going away makes her smile like that.

"Yes, *carai*. The Remasian Council chose you. Says you are the only one the young leader seemed to like."

"They *were* watching us!"

"I watched you too." Her words are so simple, but they say so much more. She practically glows. "I also watched them, the council members, and the current leader. They nodded and made notes in your favor, *babila*. I knew they would pick you before they commed today."

But why the quiet after we left the House of Decision. Why didn't she smile like this and make me feel better? I'd thought I failed, and it hurt.

"You needed to learn a little humility, *daja*." Mim speaks as if she reads my mind. She does that a lot. Makes me wonder if she's a secret telepath. "Confidence is good, but you can't believe that you will always succeed. It makes you less hungry to exceed expectations."

Oh.

And it all crashes down on me.

I didn't fail. I passed. My parents are proud because I'm going to do something no mage has ever done. I'll get the best training, learn novel skills, be better connected than Mim and Fasa put together.

And I'll be erased from this house.

Tomorrow.

"It's okay to cry for now, *daja*. Tears are for this house. But tomorrow, no more. You are representing the Lilias mage line. You've been accepted by the highest form of this planet's government to rise and be even greater in one of the strongest planetary alliances in the world."

Tears flow from her eyes too, and I nearly fall over. Mim is crying. She comes to me and wraps her arms around my body. A hug.

We don't do hugs.

"Fasa and I will take you tomorrow."

They're both going to see me off. Mages who leave home are never seen off.

I rest my head on Mim's shoulder and cry. One last time.

Because after this, I'm special. The representative of the Lilias mage line. There's nothing to cry about. This is what everyone wants.

I need to want it to.

And after this hug, I'll want it.

~*~

DAWN IS COLD. THE SUN takes a few *jewels* before it actually warms the Third Dome. It'll be hot by noon, but I won't be here to feel it. Fasa and Mim shift in and out of the house, supervising the packing of my things. They give me more weapons from the basement closets, more texts to study. I sit at the meal table, snacking on cold cheese cubes. Thinking about how bare my room was after I'd come back from my bath. It'll be used for something else soon. Not my mine anymore.

A heavy thud at my side signals Dalton coming to join me. I frown at him. He's never loud or heavy. He's got bags under his eyes and his hair is a rodent's nest. Still sick then.

"You look like beast barf." I push my cheese plate toward him.

He ignores it. "I'm glad you're leaving."

Not surprised. With me gone, he's going to

be a Viper. "Who will you fight, though?" I ask.

Dalton taps the table. "Mim."

"You're taking my place."

"*My* place. They never really decided which one of us was going to go."

I snort. "You can't be serious."

His glare tells me that he is. Oh. I didn't know he thought he had a chance before now. I tilt my head. "Do you think you're better?"

"Than you?" Dalton huffs. "Of course I am."

Well, *feep*. "But Mim and Fasa say—"

"The same things to me when you stop paying attention. When you lose interest, your senses dull. We don't have any competition here but each other. Mim and Fasa tell us both we're the one they're proud of, to make us work harder to stay the golden kid." He coughs into the crook of his elbow. "I hear it all, and you should too. It's not hard to keep yourself in the know. Work on that."

His tone is light, almost gentle. "Dalton?" Maybe he's dying because I've never ever heard him sound like that. Like he cares about me.

He clears his throat and looks anywhere but at me. "I'm glad you're leaving. Living with you *plores*. But don't embarrass me, okay? When I see you again, I want to fight you and you better still be as good as me."

Shock keeps me silent. I think my brother is being nice. A hell must be freezing over. I nod at him, and he takes the cheese I offered. We sit, eating, as our parents finish packing me up.

When the time comes, I leave with Mim and Fasa. Dalton stays at home to study. I watch the house shrink in the back window of Mim's railer. Memorizing its round shape and flat roof. Etching the tall trees in the front yard into my brain and noting how the house disappears when we're a *ka* away—its magical barrier hiding it from plain sight, and from me for the last time.

Fasa, who's not piloting, pats my head, and I turn around, to look straight.

FRACTIONS

~*~

THE TRAM RIDE IS A blur. I'm hustled between Mim and Fasa on silver paved streets, around tall buildings and past manicured parks. Everything is neat and uniform, the recycled air smells stale. The building we end up in is so tall I can't see where it ends when I lean my head back. A man in military cargos greets us at the main glass doors and leads us in. Everything inside shines like its polished on the *jewel*. The walls are gray, lined with portraits of leaders. Some resemble the little leader I met in a way, others don't. The styles of clothing change with each image. I'm walking through a history lesson.

"Come, *babila*." Fasa looks over his shoulder at me.

I'm falling behind. I hurry to catch up, walking between Fasa and Mim as we follow the soldier down another endless hall. Doors with glowing panels come into view and the man stops at one and turns to me.

"Press your palm against the panel, young lady. Spread your fingers wide. It needs to read your print and sync to your biorhythms. This will be your room, until you're old enough to be on your own." The man's voice is rough, like he gargles glass on his lunch breaks.

"Go on, *daja*." Mim touches my shoulder.

I push my palm against the panel beside the door and hold still as heat runs over my calluses. The square glows white and the door slides upward to reveal a plain room. Light blue walls, a four-corner bed with white sheets, no top blanket. A duraplastic desk and chair. No windows. There's a door in back that I walk to, and open. A tiny bathroom, with a cleansing stall, sink and waster, gleams white.

"It's so clean." I shut the bathroom door and turn to survey my new room again. Mim and Fasa knock on walls and check under the bed. Standard searches for hexes and traps.

But Remasians don't do magic like that. Who could curse the place?

The soldier stands in the doorway, seeming unsure what to do, as he watches my parents pulling back sheets and opening desk drawers. There's a closet built into the wall. Mim opens it and starts in on the towels and sheets.

The soldier clears his throat and Fasa and Mim turn as a unit to stare at him.

The man goes pale, hands twitching toward the energy rifle clipped to his belt, but he doesn't draw. "Uh, the girl's things are being brought in. You can stay and help her unpack, but visiting hours are strict around here for civilian guests."

"Are you telling us that we should prepare to take our leave?" Fasa's voice is so deep. I never notice it until other men speak around him. Fasa's baritone is distinct.

And it unnerves so many people. The soldier swallows. "Yessir."

"Will we know our daughter's schedule?" Mim asks.

The soldier shakes his head. "I'm sorry."

Neither Mim nor Fasa seem surprised about that. It'd be pretty stupid to tell outsiders plans for your soldiers. Which means I won't be able to tell Mim and Fasa what I'm doing. Not really. And visiting hours...

"You can only come at certain times?" I ask. Because they're busy. If they can't come when they're free, there might not ever be a time when they can see me.

"You won't have time to see us, *daja*," Mim says, gesturing for me to come to her. I move to stand in front of her and Fasa. She takes my shoulders. "You'll be training."

She doesn't sound sad. This is an honor. I should agree with her and smile and tell them goodbye. But my hand shakes as I reach for hers. I bite my lip. "Mim?"

"No crying." Fasa is firm. "Lilias mages do not cry or snivel. You are going to be the best of us. Reflect that always. We will see each other when we can. It might not be as often as you would like, but you truly will be too busy to notice. I want you to be stronger, faster, and skilled in five new weapons before

I see you next, because I assure you that Dalton will be."

"Dalton could be here. He's as good as I am."

"The Remasian Council asked for you and the leader apparent chose you," Fasa says. He rubs his cleanly shaven chin. "Dalton would be worthy here, but now his path is chosen, as is yours. You will both make us proud, Desired One."

My heart pounds and my face and ears burn, as they always do when Fasa compliments me. I want to keep this feeling, and the only way to do it is... I bow. "Yes, Fasa."

He pats my head and Mim plants a kiss in my hair.

"That's a good, *daja oir*"—our beautiful daughter.

~*~

THEY STAY FOR ANOTHER *JEWEL*. Helping me put away my things when my boxes arrive. Helping me set my wards. Then, they leave without a backward glance. I stand in the doorway, watching until I can't see them anymore. I go to my bed and lie on my back, staring at the boring blue ceiling, stomach quivering. Mind alive with thoughts of Dalton, Mim, and Fasa, and what I have to do on the path Fasa said was chosen for me.

I take a deep breathe, holding it for a few *wisps*.

In the bathing chamber at home, on the morning Mim first brought me to this place, she said this would be my first and maybe only job as a mage.

I'm here to do what no other mage outside of a royal appointment has done before. Work without a contract within an army, serve a leader. Gain influence with powerful people. Be someone my parents can brag about from far away.

I exhale, long and slow. Seeing my family's faces in my mind, feeling Fasa's pats, Mim's kiss, and hearing Dalton's voice be gentle. I see my old room emptied out, the bathing chamber, the meal table, and finally the shrinking image of our house as it vanishes behind a protective barrier. Gone.

I repeat the word 'Gone'. And I'll keep repeating it until I can think it without burning eyes and a hurting stomach.

"Lilias mages don't cry or snivel."

I exhale again.

Gone.

My eyes still burn, but my stomach doesn't hurt as much.

A knock on the door. I spring off the bed, landing in a crouch. "Who's out there." There's a panel on the inside of the door too. It glows and shows me two kids outside the door. The little leader and the nymph. Evan and Adonis.

"Stop looking at us and come out," Evan says through the com.

I sneer. "Who says I'm looking at you?"

"I heard you say, 'who's out there?'." He puts his hands on his hips. "Come out. I want to see your fire again and I want to teach you a game."

And here I thought I'd never find out what game the little leader had wanted to play with me. I stretch my hand toward the panel to open the door and pause.

Going out to join them, to play and practice fire, feels strange. Not bad, but like truly shutting a door on something and walking through another. I'd never do this at home. Go play. It'd be frowned at, spat on. But the house that disappeared isn't my home anymore.

I chew my lower lip and exhale one more time. Long and slow.

Gone.

Only my eyes burn.

"I'm coming out!" I press my hand against the panel, and the door to my new path opens wide and says...

"It's about time! Come on. We've gotta steal some snacks first. Follow me!"

I do. And like my parents, I don't look back.

FRACTIONS

~*~

NOW

SUNSET DOES NOTHING TO LOWER the temperature of this slime-bucket planet. I hike back to the glorified shack the Mujbonian tribunal put us up in, moping sweat off my brow with the back of my hand. A heavy sack of silver smacks against my lower back. I'd fashioned a knapsack out of the burlap bag Shopkeeper Wique sold me at a discount.

I kick open the rickety wooden door and step into the single room unit, big enough to house all four of us, me, Evan, Adonis, and Jalee, but not large enough to keep us from getting on each other's nerves for long. Evan and Adonis look up from a game of cards they're playing at a round table. Small, gold squares, Evan's new belt and a corked vial of something purple sit in the center of the table.

"You guys gambling without me?" I sling my bag of silver on the floor by the mattress I'd claimed on our first night here. The only nice thing this crusty place has to offer is four separate mattresses for us to sleep on. We pushed them into respective corners. The only other furniture is the round table with chairs and a single couch that slumps to the right.

"Nobody knew where you were." Evan looks me up and down and cocks his head to stare at my loot bag. "You found silver?"

"Yeah."

"You found something else too." Adonis's voice is a cool. It never sounds sly or teasing, but I know him well enough now to get what he means.

"Yeah, a shopkeeper. He's kinda cute. And hey, if we stay here a little longer, I might find him again tomorrow." Wique *had* taken me to his favorite fishing hole. We didn't fish, though.

"*Fip*. You had a date? That's it?" Evan groans and takes a heavy obsidian ring off his

117

thumb, tossing it as Adonis who catches it in a fist. "*Fip!*"

"What? What'd you bet on?" I ask, coming to the table. There's a bowl of crunchy snacks on one of the empty chairs. There are four seats, one dragged in for each of us. Mighty kind of the Mujbonians to think of chairs and mattresses.

I snag a snack and pop it in my mouth. Corn powder coats my tongue. I tug on Evan's messy braid. "What'd you bet, *gak mopi?*"

He grunts. "That you were burying a Mujbonian shopkeeper in a swamp after they tried to sell you *pidgy* goods."

My mouth opens at that. "You thought I murdered somebody?" I might be insulted. Or not. I did consider killing Wique.

I gaze between him and Adonis. Adonis, the one who had faith in me, shrugs. I glare at his cousin—my little leader. The *gak mopi* grins, all dimples and bright eyes.

"I had a request for your pardon all written out and signed. You would have been out of Mujbonian lock up before they turned a key.

Or whatever they have. I don't think there is a jail."

And that warm feeling—the one I used to feel when my parents spoke of their pride in me—comes from this little *pidge* being, "My brother! You'd abuse your political power to get me out of jail?"

I wrap an arm around his neck and squeeze until he grunts again, patting my arm, a signal for me to let go so he can breathe. Strangers would think I was choking him. But that's how I do hugs.

Evan coughs as I plop down in the last chair and ask to be dealt into the game.

I love games.

Adonis gathers up all the cards and re-shuffles.

"What are you wagering?" Evan asks. "I don't need your silver."

I snort. Like I was going to give him that. I dig in my boot, extracting Dalton's stiletto and setting it on the table. Its milky white blade catches the light and Evan frowns at it.

"Did you just get that?"

"Yeah." I tap its leather hilt. "A gift."

119

"From your shopkeeper?" Evan touches the handle of the dagger and picks it up to eyeball.

I shake my head and take the cards Adonis gives me.

"From who then?" Adonis slides the stiletto from Evan. He turns it over in his hands. "This looks like—"

"A Viper's blade." I take it back, twirling it between my fingers. Handling it is as easy as the smiles I'd once wanted from Mim. It fits in my hand like it's made for me, or for someone who's always been as good as me.

Evan's eyes go wide. "Whoa, does that mean..."

I shake my head again. "It was sold to the shopkeeper by a Viper. The shopkeeper let me take it, so it's an indirect gift. From Dalton."

"Your brother Dalton?" Evan puts down his cards. "He was here?"

I nod. "And now he's gone." Gone.

"Why would he sell this?" Evan asks. "I thought Vipers got buried with these things."

120

I shrug. "Not like I can ask him. Haven't seen him in *revs*." Gone.

"Do you want to try to find him after this? We've got some free time coming up." Evan crunches on some snacks and offers me the bowl. He's frowning again, at me. Probably trying to figure out if I'm okay. He's funny like that. He should know better.

I'm fine. I closed that door a long time ago. That house, that family, that life is gone.

I grab a fistful of snacks and shove them in my mouth. In between crunches, I say, "No, I don't want to find that *critch-cratch*. Let's use that free time to play."

"There's a bar on Taleen a guy I was with kept talking about. It has black ice liquor that catches fire in your stomach." Adonis drops a card on the table. "You gambling that dagger or keeping it?"

I laugh in his direction. "Careful, you'll pass your word quota for the day." Most people think Adonis doesn't talk, but really? He says a lot more to people he knows.

A little leader told me that a long time ago.

I sigh at the stiletto. If I wager it and lose,

it'll be gone. As everything from that time in my life should be.

But.

Why would Dalton sell this and why would I end up with it? Is this one of those instances where I should pay more attention? Wique might know more. I could ask deeper questions tomorrow. If we stay.

I exhale. Can't recall their faces as well as I used to. Can't remember the last time I heard *daja mir*. I can remember a brother who told me I'd better still be as good as him when we crossed paths again. A brother who'd obviously ditched his path as a Viper.

Gone, but not.

I tuck the stiletto back in my boot. "Nah, I'm not gambling this one. How about a barrette instead?"

I unpin my hair, and the game starts.

~*~

THE NEXT DAY, WE STAY and I return
to Upo's to ask Wique about a rogue mage.

END

A SPOILER BONUS: THE PINK RIVER

Maiden Imari

Author's Note: This short story is a spoiler for an event that happens in BOOK III, THE SECOND ENDGAME. Be warned that reading it might ruin a big reveal, but I couldn't resist writing a love story. If you don't mind blatant hints at what's to come in a story, please enjoy this piece.

I HATE AND LOVE WHEN he smiles.
The expression drags me back to a distant
past I am cursed to relive in nightmares and
long moments of silence. I do not sleep more
than a few *jewels* a night and maintain
constant levels of noise as treatment for my
chronic condition of a broken heart. The
patchwork organ beats, pumping blood
through a body that has not aged since its
twentieth *revolution* more than an epoch ago.
I raised pups that grew to be large old hounds
that died fat and loved and left me with
generations of new pups to care for. I
nurtured gardens, seedlings that sprouted
into the great forest that surrounds my
personal cottage. All to bide my time until
Corin returned. Kahanna is a liar, but I
trusted that he would come back because it
was part of Her wager, a factor She had to let
govern itself.

And now he is here, and that smile is the

same and different, because his soul fuels another being. That Evan Lauduethe is this age, the age when Corin and I fell in love, and now I am old, and he is not, hurts like a dull axe chipping away at flesh and bone. That I could possibly love this boy more than Corin is a newly sharpened dagger through the heart.

"You're really going to eat all of that?" Evan stares at me from across the wooden table. Three empty bowls rest in front of him. He runs a finger along the rim of one and sucks fish juice off it.

The motion itself is disgusting, but the fish juice is delicious. This tiny cottage restaurant, with its brown wooden floors and square tables and benches for chairs, is excellent.

I pull my second bowl of tangy fish porridge closer to me and stab my large spoon into the chunky yellow mound of starch and meat. "I will not share with you. Order a fourth bowl."

He groans, having the nerve to look

frustrated. "The natives already think I'm a *gub*. I have an image to maintain."

Those wide green eyes of his shine with mirth and the corners of his full lips twitch, revealing quick flashes of dimples. Loose curls, a dark gold that is almost brown, frame that face, Corin's but not. Evan seems younger than Corin ever was. His features a bit more rounded, hair more unruly, eyes larger, lashes darker, frame shorter, thinner. His fae heritage is apparent in his looks, magic, and mannerisms. Corin had a trickle of Breed Blood in his veins that heated his magic, but the world never sang for him as it does for his second coming.

"If you keep staring at me like that, I'm going to steal your porridge," Evan says. He reaches for my bowl and I whack his hand with my spoon.

He grunts in surprise, yanking his hand back and gaping at me. "Has anyone ever told you you're mean?"

"No one on Lenore would ever tell me." None would insult a Maiden of Lenore, until recently. "Before you and the other

Champions joined us, I had not seen a face that was not green since..."

"Since I died the first time?" He waves a hand at a pink-skinned waitress in a blue frock and she nods and spins on a heel toward the kitchen.

"Yes." I spoon porridge into my mouth, savoring the spicy sweet taste while marveling over him. He is so blunt and forever in motion. He says what he thinks and readies his fists to fight if it causes a problem. Corin was more cautious, a charming diplomat who managed to maintain an aura of innocence. He was a sip of cool water. Refreshing, pleasant, life-bringing. Evan is a fizzy bottle of hot seltzer. Maddening, delicious, energy-inducing.

Evan picks up his large spoon and spins it over a knuckle. "Are we still hiking that hill after this? Or will you be too full. Old people nap after big meals, right?"

He winks at me.

"I hear that some old people do." I take another bite of porridge. "But I am not that old yet, and you *still* will not have any of my porridge."

He sniffs as if insulted and flips the spoon off his knuckle into one of the bowls. It clatters and he chuckles. Music begins, a three-piece band of string players strum large wooden instruments with long necks and triangular bases. The cottage-restaurant is perpetually open, but several *jewels* before dawn does not draw in a large crowd. Five other customers plus the musicians occupy the establishment, and those five people spring out of their chairs, and fall into the formation of a group dance. They wobble and sway, undoubtedly under the influence of the complementary ale that comes with the fish porridge. Evan had waved it away in favor of sweet milk. I take tiny sips from my brown, wooden mug, wishing I had gotten sweet milk too. But the recommendation given to me by the lady medic was to have the porridge with beer.

I want the full experience and memories, because I do not have these types of recollections. Enjoying myself in a dirty restaurant, eating local fare and using utensils that have touched other tongues and lips. Everything brought to me on Lenore was fresh, specially prepared and served to me using plates, bowls and spoons crafted for me.

The table moves as Evan gets to his feet. He claps to the rhythm of the music, observing the dancers before he joins the line, fumbling through steps before he catches on. The five drunk dancers laugh and pat his back and shoulders when they shuffle through moves. The musicians smile and increase their tempo.

I watch, savoring the way the overhead lighting plays with the contrast of Evan's bright hair against his dark skin, and the way his hips swivel and his feet kick and tap out fancy counts as if he has done this dance all his life. Corin also danced well. Predicting the patterns of choreographed motions came easily to him. He was meant to dance, but he used that talent to fight instead.

A woman, young and pretty, leaps at Evan, and he catches her. It is part of the dance.

He spins her before she moves on to another partner to repeat the same move. I glare at the way his eyes follow her body with too much interest. A feeling rustles in my stomach and I try to smother it with another lump of porridge. He can look at whomever he wants. He is not mine, after all. Corin was mine. Evan is... He just is.

"I wouldn't let my man dance with Keilany." The pink-skinned waitress sets a steaming bowl of fish porridge on the table next to Evan's stack of empty bowls. She raises a green eyebrow at me. Her equally green hair is pulled up in a braided bun. "She broke up with her boyfriend six *cycles* ago and has been here every night to make him jealous."

"Is the previous boyfriend here?"

"He's the one making your porridge," the waitress says. "Might want to tell your boyfriend not to order another bowl."

"He is not my boyfriend." It aches to speak the truth.

"Oh?" The waitress seems confused. "I just thought...with the way you two are with

131

each other that... Are you waiting to ask him or for him to ask you?"

"Ask him what?" I murmur. I watch as Evan laughs with Keilany and a tall man with well-groomed stubble over his chin and cheeks. The musicians strike up a new tune and the man extends a hand to Evan who shrugs and takes it.

"Hm." The waitress.

I look back to her eyes on the dance floor too. She places a hand on a wide hip. "Or perhaps you like him, and he likes everyone else. You shouldn't put up with that. Give him an ultimatum."

I chuckle. "It is not like that. He and I are...old friends. We had something once, but that time has passed and now... now, I take pleasure in knowing that he can be happy." And I can ensure he stays this way.

Those words hurt less, and I can smile.

The waitress looks dubious. "You sure about that?"

No. "Yes. Thank you."

The woman shrugs. "Do you think your

not-boyfriend would appreciate more koca milk?"

I shake my head and she leaves, obviously paying attention to the dance floor as she makes her way to the kitchen. Evan accepts clingy hugs from Keilany and the male he had danced with and abandons the dance floor. He drops into his seat and digs into the new bowl of porridge as if he had not devoured three bowls earlier. Amusement keeps me from being disgusted. I look over his bowed head to see the male who had been part of Evan and Keilany's group scowling at me.

Is he jealous?

I giggle and Evan glances at me. "What's funny?"

"One of your dance partners is not happy with me."

Evan chews and tosses a look over his shoulder. He turns back, swallowing, then laughing. "That guy wants me to come back tomorrow, so he can teach me another dance."

"Is he...interested?" I press. The man is dancing again.

"Interested?" Evan licks his spoon. "Yeah. He asked if I was with you, and when I said, 'it's complicated', he got a little hopeful."

And there is that feeling in my chest again. I am jealous. "Are *you* interested?" I attempt to look as if I do not care.

Evan gazes at me from under his lashes—and what long, dark lashes they are. Corin's lashes were never that thick. "Do I hear jealousy?"

I cannot say 'no', so I say nothing.

He laughs like a sprite, wicked and loud. The sound is as infectious as it is nerve-wracking. I bop the top of his head with my spoon. He snatches it from my hand and dips into my porridge, taking a bite. I gape at him and pull my bowl away so he cannot get anymore. "I told you that you could not have any!"

"You did." He smiles, close-mouthed, with cheeks full of porridge—my porridge.

"*Gak mopi.*" I hold out my hand for my spoon.

"Why should I give it back? You hit me."

"Honestly." I reach out and grab my spoon, gasping when he does not let go. All right. Two can play games. I release the head of the spoon and get to my feet. He watches me, eyes sparkling with mischief, then confusion as I rush around the table.

Corin was ticklish under his arms and around his belly. I attack the underarms first and drop to his middle as he tries to fight me off.

His counterattacks are weak as he falls prey to reflexive laughter. Reclaiming my spoon is easy as his fingers go slack. I tuck the utensil in my pocket with one hand while continuing to tickle his belly.

I yelp as he spins around on the bench, grabbing me and pulling me onto his lap. He holds me, wrapping his arms around my waist as he bows his head over my shoulder, laughing breathlessly.

"You're going to pay for that."

"I am not afraid," I sing.

"You mean that." His breath is hot on my neck, his thick curls tickle my cheek. He smells like antibacterial military soap and outdoors. And he feels like...I lean back into him, needing to be closer.

Niobe-va, I miss you, Corin.

I tense in his embrace for just a moment. Because, sometimes, it just does not feel right. However, I also *know* who I am with, and I am sure he has decided how he feels about me. The conflict that used to war behind his mossy green eyes has not been there since we were together on his ship. He does not love me. His looks do not smolder as Corin's had when our eyes met, but there is a gentle fondness and simmering attraction that I accept as permission to do many things.

I giggle as his lips tease my neck, not kissing, just brushing up the column of my spine, and then he blows the hair at the nape of my neck and—I shriek as he tickles me there. I roll my neck away and leap off his lap. "You childish imp!"

"You started it." He leans back, elbows on the table, as he laughs.

Huffing, I grab my loose hair, weaving it

into a single plait to match his, glowering at him all the while. I feel eyes on us and figure the entire restaurant is paying attention. Heavy cologne that smells of dark wood and sweet spice clouds my head. The man from the dance floor moves past me and slides beside Evan on his bench. He grins with a mouth full of straight white teeth and touches Evan's shoulder.

Evan turns to him, expression curious, and the man says, "I cannot let you get away without exchanging information."

Evan blinks, laughter gone, but he still looks friendly. He shrugs and reaches into one of the many pockets of his stiff military pants and pulls out a palm-sized device—a compal. Everyone outside of Lenore seems to have one of these things, as the stubble-faced man also produces one from the side pocket of his silk pants.

The man—he is older than Evan by a few years. Or maybe he is not. I am not a good judge of how old people are based on looks or mannerisms. Some species look nauseatingly young for centuries, and others invest in potions, treatments, and magic to stave off wrinkles and other signs of being beyond their prime. If I had a choice, I would rather have the mature appearance of a matron. My own people treat me as a child due to cheeks still plump with baby-fat.

"Nice to meet you, Yaqi," Evan says, patting the man on the knee.

Yaqi, who is semi-handsome, sharp featured and dark-haired, smiles, then glances at his device. Evan chuckles as Yaqi's dark brown eyes go comically wide.

"Y-you..."

Evan beams. "You don't keep up with the news."

"I... Not... I try to limit my viewing of world affairs, your... uh..."

"Evan is fine," Evan says. "And..." Devilry gleams in his bright eyes. "May I introduce you to Maiden Imari of Lenore?"

Yaqi's jaw drops as his head whips to me. He launches to his feet, bowing deep at the waist. "*Avaristi-va*, I apologize, ma'am! I am deeply honored to be in your presence! How presumptuous of me to—to..." He turns on

Evan, who is positively howling with laughter.

If I did not know better, I would think he was the one who consumed ale tonight.

Oh, poor Yaqi looks hurt, as if a cruel joke is being played on him.

"Do not apologize to me and ignore this awful troll!" I take Yaqi's surprisingly soft hands in mine and smile. He starts in surprise at being touched. The reverence does not fade from his look, but he no longer seems insulted.

"You are not what I expected a Maiden to be." His deep voice is velvety, and I hold back a thrill of pleasure at its sound, at his interest as he studies me. He looks at me as if I am someone to respect, but also...maybe...as a woman. "You can't be as young as you appear and here you are in a terrible tavern in a dusty old river town eating... did you have the fish porridge?"

"And the ale," I say. "Very delicious, though I had to fight to finish my own portions. Some beings do not understand that everything is not meant to be shared." I gesture at Evan, who is wiping his eyes with the backs of his hands.

"You and Leader Lauduethe are here with the armies! There was a party earlier, that you missed, all about our win. This is a bit of an after party for those of us who can't sleep until first sunrise."

My stomach flips. First sunrise. The beginning of a new day for these people, and the beginning of an end to so many things for Champions of Order.

But now is not the time for those thoughts.

"It is a fine after party," I say and Yaqi grins at me.

"May I?" My eyes widen as he takes my hand and brings it his lips. "Lovely to meet you. You and..." he looks over his shoulder at Evan...who is eating my porridge. "You two should take a boat down the river. At this time of night, the moon makes it sparkle. And there are blood -red nightvine blossoms that open their petals lining the shore and shuttergrits with glowing wings. In fact, if you go to the East Dock, tell Mamoreet you are good with Yaqi. He'll get you the best boat." He narrows his eyes at Evan. "Make him paddle, because..." Yaqi frowns. "Was he toying with me?"

I shake my head, and give a warm, yet long-suffering sigh. "I doubt it. He is many things, but misleading is not one of them. You should contact him later. He is not always so..." I bite my lower lip. Because I do not know how Evan always is. Sometimes, he is serious. He can be dedicated, methodical, and sharp when it comes to duty. Other times, he plays with puppies, dances with strangers, steals food, and is a young man full of bright laughter, mischief, and boundless energy.

What would he be like if there were no wars, or curses, or prophecies?

But if there were no prophecy or curse, would this young man even exist? When Corin died, there would have been no magic to recycle his soul. So, in a way, I have Kahanna to thank for the maddening creature now sipping my unattended ale.

"You love him." Yaqi lowers his voice as he leans closer to me.

My sharp intake of breath almost chokes me. I clear my throat and nod. "I do."

"You'll enjoy the boat, ma'am."

"Please call me Imari." He straightens, gazing down in shock. I smile at him. "And call that intolerable *gak mopi* Evan."

Yaqi's full smile reveals deep dimples in his stubbled cheeks. He bows and kisses my hand again. "Enjoy your boat, Imari."

Imari. Someone who is not one of my sisters or another Champion called me by my name. It has been too many centuries since I was just 'that girl' Imari. The one who was hopeless at sweeping and dusting, and who loved to roll down grass hills in nothing but coveralls and bare feet and laugh at quarreling tree cats and naughty children hiding in the woods to skip their daily lessons. I was very good at skulking about, camouflaging myself in shrubbery and earth, to world-watch. People, animals, everything that makes up what constitutes reality was fascinating then. I fancied myself a cataloger. I knew about every affair in the temple, every scandal in town, but knew little of temple rituals, chants, and hymns.

I was the worst temple girl. And now, the worst Maiden.

An arm drapes itself over my shoulders and I gasp, nearly jumping out of my skin. Evan peers down at me, a dark brow raised. I swallow at how truly beautiful he is to me, at how I see Corin also frowning through his eyes.

"I was lost in thought. Sorry."

He hums. "I scared Yaqi away."

"He might contact you anyway." I lean against his side. "He says we should take a boat ride. We could do that instead of swim."

Evan wrinkles his nose. "I thought the idea of a hike canceled out that pink river stuff."

I tilt my head, momentarily confused at his reluctance. "You..." inherited the magic of ember sprites. They hate water. I giggle.

"What?"

"You have an aversion to conquer and we shall do it tonight! Come. We have a boat to catch!"

He gapes at me as I duck under his arm

and dig silver squares out of my pants pocket. I lay them on the table and wave to our waitress who leans by the kitchen door, watching us, a mystified expression on her face. Perhaps Yaqi shared with her our identities. I gaze around to see other people in the tavern pretending not to study us. Their heads turn in opposite directions whenever I look at them. Inconspicuous they are not.

I grab Evan by the short sleeve of his shirt. "Let us go!"

We leave the tavern with the sound of string music and gossip at our backs. But above it all, I remember Yaqi's kiss to the hand and his use of my first name without a title and feel freer somehow. The warm air makes loose tendrils of hair stick to my cheeks and sweat pepper my brow, not a perfect night, but more wonderful due to its imperfections. Spicy fish porridge and chimney smoke flavor the air, making it almost tasty to breathe.

I take Evan's hand and swing our arms. "Can you swim?"

His look is moody. "Yeah."

"Will you swim skyclad with me?"

"Now, who's the imp?"

I laugh, and he lets me continue to swing our arms, as we journey to the pink river.

~*~

THE WATER GLISTENS A MILKY rose hue. Evan gives it dubious looks as we reach a gray wooden dock surrounded by bobbing boats made for two to four passengers. A portly man with a bald face, no eyebrows, no eyelashes, grins at us with large yellowing teeth.

"Leader Lauduethe and Maiden Imari." He bows at the waist. "My friend commed ahead, and I polished this one just for you."

I blink as the man motions to one of the boats. It looks like the others, but I suppose its insides are a trifle cleaner. Evan sighs and peers at the water again. "People use this water to disinfect wounds. If we fall in—"

"Jump in," I supply.

He stares at me, then at who I am assuming is Mamoreet. "How much will it burn?"

Mamoreet seems amused. His voice lilts. "The water tingles against the skin, very healing. The chemical compound caused by the properties of the riverbed is diluted by the water. Where the river is deepest is the best place to swim. Keep your eyes covered, though." He produces two pairs of googles from the breast pocket of his fitted shirt. The thin material strains across his chest and belly, threatening to pop.

I take the goggles. "Thank you!"

"You'll be quite alone. I won't lend out any more boats tonight...though it truly is the best time out on the Rwasana."

"The river's name?"

Mamoreet nods. "It means 'healing' in Canti. And 'peace' in Terp." Canti and Terp, two of the dominant dialects on this planet. "The bench seats inside the boat are hollow.

146

Lift the lids, there are towels and canteens of water."

"You and Yaqi are too kind," I say.

Mamoreet shakes his head and bows his head to me. He is not a tall man, he may have an *iut* less than Evan, but he is larger than me. I do not feel intimidated, instead I feel...

"May I?" Mamoreet asks.

I nod and let Mamoreet brace my forearms and bow his head again. "You and the leader are here to save us all. The least any of us can do is let you have a boat and some water. If you had let Sania know who you were, your meal would have been given to you."

I shake my head. "Do not..." Do not give me things for that. Not when you would have never been born if Kahanna had kept her word to me, and I would not have cared. Shame lowers my eyes to my dirty boots.

Evan moves to stand beside us, looking at Mamoreet's hands on my arms with a slight frown. Mamoreet releases me and bows to Evan but does not move to grab his arms.

"What lives in this water?" Evan asks.

147

"River eels, and a few fingi serpents. Harmless, but delicious when stewed."

I pass Evan a pair goggles and grin at his annoyed scowl. "He thinks the river will eat him," I say to Mamoreet as if I am telling a very loud secret.

Evan grunts and looks to Mamoreet. "Thanks for the boat. How much—"

Mamoreet shakes his head and nods to the boat he cleaned for us. I make my way to it and hop off the deck into the small boat. It bobs and I sway, before sitting down on a hard seat. Mamoreet passes Evan a set of oars. Where he got them from, I do not know. Evan takes the oars and steps down into the boat, sitting quickly as Mamoreet unties us from the dock.

The river's current is gentle but firm. Our boat drifts from shore, taking us down a wide, milky pink path that winds through foliage and hanging red vines with red, slender petaled blossoms. Tiny insects with glittery green and gold wings flutter near the flowers, like miniature lanterns in the wildness. I wave to the disappearing form of

Mamoreet on the dock and smile when he waves back.

"You make friends easily," Evan says. He sets the paddles on the floor of the boat, seeming content to let the river pull us where it wants. "Didn't know you socialized all that well."

"What is that supposed to mean?"

Evan shrugs. "Well, you were kind of isolated for a very long time. Sometimes, people- skills get a little rusty. But I think you do better when people don't bow to you. That guy on the dock..."

"You heard what he said?"

"About us saving them?" Evan looks at the sky. "Yeah."

"I—"

"Heard what you were starting to say too."

"Yes."

We float, the white moon making the rose water shimmer. The air smells faintly of disinfectant and...and sweet oil. I noticed the same aroma on the soldier who told me I had to try fish porridge and to see the river at night. Nightvine blossoms must be used in local perfume and lotion.

"We'll save these people," Evan says after a long while. "That guy won't be wrong."

He appears resigned as he stares at the water, a tired hero. I see Corin hunched over maps, wiping weary, shadowed eyes, draining large cups of kava and chewing thrys root to stay energized. He had plans for after the war. He wanted to travel with teams dedicated to rebuilding what the fighting destroyed. He thought he'd be offered a position on the Remasian Council or even invited to be on one of the Allegiance Councils. And maybe he would have achieved the latter. Rema never appreciates its leaders. They are pawns, not rulers. Weapons, not people.

Kahanna has no place in Her new world for all twelve of the Remasian councilors, and no room for the Zaran Parliament. Theorne and Viveen of Rema secured their seats at Her side by suggesting the *rax*—Corin's future bridle—the Mark that would control generations of Remasian leaders until the final Four were born.

"What does it feel like when..." We sit knee to knee, bodies facing each other. He looks beyond me, undoubtedly peering into the trees, and I reach out, cupping a hand behind the back of his neck and running two fingers down the top ridges of his spine. The Mark, the swirling, beautiful lines and scrawls of text and symbols, denoting Evan as Rema's leader, and giving the damnable coordinates to a Stone he had uncovered in the wrong place at the wrong time.

He catches my hand behind his neck, holding it, gazing at me. My breath catches at the intensity of his stare, my cheeks warm. He lets go as I rise and move both of my hands to his shoulders for balance then situate myself on his lap, straddling his knees.

He rests his warm, sticky forehead against mine. "Why do you want to know how it feels?"

"Because..." Corin had not been able to tell me. I had watched him crumple twice as the *rax* was activated by Viveen or Theorne. I want to understand his pain.

"It's like lightning under my skin, shooting through every nerve in my body." He sounds absent. "And right when you think you'll finally die this time, it stops. And everything's so *fipping* quiet after. I can't hear, or see color, or taste bitter or sweet for hours." He stokes my hair, never looking away. "But when I can get up again, and see, and hear, and maybe taste every flavor I lost, I go back to work."

Corin had always gone back to work, until he could not. Until he was too mad to remember to bathe or eat. In the end, he even lost my name. His brothers he knew, he cried for them and stared at me like I was a nobody. And that day, when he looked at me with blank eyes and said he had to go, I knew I would never see him again.

I kiss Evan's sweaty cheek. "You will never feel the wrath of that curse on your skin again."

"Oh?" He looks half-amused, half-melancholy.

He has to know what is to come will not be entirely what he wants. At least, I do not think it will be entirely what he wants. I hope.

Because...I want him to love me.

I run my lips along the smooth line of his cheek until they find his hot mouth. His full lips part and I slide in for a kiss. He kisses better than Corin, holds me more firmly, touches more confidently. Corin was my only. I only knew what *he* felt like, how *he* did it. And now I know that perhaps Corin might have been able to say the same about me being his only then too. We learned together, clumsy, exciting, and painful but beautiful. Evan is educated, and there is nothing clumsy about anything he does.

And after, he agrees to dive into the water with me.

~*~

HE SITS STILL AS I finger-comb the tangles from his long hair. A little of my magic persuades a current to push us back in the direction of the dock and Mamoreet. It will be another hour before we arrive. We traveled far. The first sun will rise a half *jewel* before we set foot in camp, but there is an *airmark* between the first and second sunrise, so I am not worried about time. Not for the spell anyway. It will be done.

The time I worry about is...

His head dips, chin resting on his chest. His shoulders rise and fall in a slow, steady rhythm. I gather his glorious mane into a haphazard bun and secure it with a hair-string from my breast pocket. Then, I wrap my arms around his chest, pulling him to rest against me. I adjust his head, turning it slightly to one side so he will not wake to a crick in his neck.

I wish... I stroke curls I could not tame off his face, coiling strands around my fingers, letting them go... I wish I could have this. Midnight swims, culinary tours, trading

154

words with normal people...just floating aimlessly in a boat, snuggled close to a dear one, feeling and listening to them breathe as they sleep. Our clothed bodies are warm and somewhat damp from sweat and lingering river water. The moisture should be uncomfortable, but I like it. Just another imperfection that makes this experience all too real. Dreams omit useless details such as the tiny water bug crawling between Evan's smooth brow.

I catch the creature between my thumb and forefinger and let it crawl over my knuckles before blowing it off. It catches a breeze and drifts out to meet the glittering insects around the river blossoms.

I catalog the antiseptic smell of the water, the sweetness of the flowers, the warm moisture of a breathing body against mine, the softness of dark golden curls, the curve of a cheek, the darkness of sooty lashes. Gods beyond, I love this body and soul, no matter what name they go by.

I did not know how to fully show it before. Everyone says it. Lenorans love differently.

Only once, and even then, not many of us acknowledge that true love is selfless. Which makes me think that not many of us have truly loved. Though, sometimes, I catch Nialiah in her parlor, brewing elixirs, studying chemical combinations, with a distant look in her eyes. Like she has lost something.

I wonder if she thinks of her former husband, Sayan, who lives in another Stellar System in a different Sector. Sayan had wanted Nialiah to choose him over her vocation. I never asked her about him after that. Could not ask or eyes would be on me. Why do you want to know such strange things, Imari? What is in your mind?

I am not trusted, not after the *Prophetic Cycles*. But Kahanna cannot dismiss me.

Evan hums in his sleep, a simple song of three notes. The river blossoms tremble, their perfume sweeter for a *wisp*, before the odor lessens. A strange reaction. I have never seen nature shrink away from him before. What song is he singing? I would ask, but I would also have to wake him and...

I want him to rest. He is vulnerable in my presence. Something inside of him knows that I will keep him safe. As if it knows what must happen next. I bury my face in his hair.

If I had the power to slow time, I would extend this night and float forever, holding him like I could not hold Corin. I do not have the power to do many things. Not a strong caster, not good at brewing, not sweet-tongued enough to chant well, not dancer enough to control winds. If having power kept me important, I would have been killed with Corin.

My importance is unknown to many. Why was the little girl who could not remember her prayers Chosen by Kahanna?

Evan shifts but does not rouse. Long lashes flutter.

The dock is far, but in view now. We are almost back to where we began and closer to the end of my importance. I do not close my eyes, hating that I must blink because I miss fractions of *wisps* of this world, this life. Unlike Corin, there will not be another for me. There is no curse or prophecy of my return.

I have been alive for centuries, but I only lived for a few *jewels*. Is it ironic for an immortal to wish for more time? I kiss his hair. Why could you not come to me sooner? Before any Stones came into play. I could have watched you grow. And you might have fallen in love with me on your own, with Corin truly asleep behind your eyes.

The boat rocks softly as it hits the wooden legs of the dock. The wood creaks as footsteps near us overhead. Mamoreet stands with the rope, tying the boat to the dock. He smiles at me, and casually walks away, hands behind his back.

I whisper in Evan's ear. Something stupid and small.

He stirs slowly, and I memorize every motion, every twitch and yawn. He sits up, scratching his head and feeling the sloppy bun I made in his hair. He unspools it and pulls the messy curtain over one shoulder to deftly braid. He turns to me after he is done,

158

frowning. "You let me sleep the whole way back to shore?"

"You were tired."

"I thought you'd...want to talk more or something."

"We have talked, Evan," I say lightly. "I am pleased. This has been... the best time of my life. Thank you."

"The best time? What about when you were with... you know, him?"

"That was during a war."

"This is during a war."

"Yes." This war is different though because I know the future.

I know you live.

He gets out of the boat first and stretches out a hand to assist me. I take it and let him pull me into his arms. I enjoy a hug and, after thanking Mamoreet, we walk back to town and find our borrowed rover.

I operate the controls, loving the rumble of the motor and the way the vehicle bounces over uneven road. I leave the shields open, letting the humidity in, so that I can smell, hear, feel, and experience the night. I glance over at Evan, appreciating his fine profile as he gazes out the open shield on his side. I only need one hand on the navigation pad to keep the rover on track, the other hand I place over his as it idles on the seat between us.

"Imari?"

"Hm?"

"Am I going to die today?"

I blink. Is he...?

"It's all right. I know spells that affect gods need mortal sacrifices. And you wouldn't do that to innocent people, not now anyway. But we need to win. And there has to be blood and I'm a Champion. The blood of a pawn of Order has to be worth a few hundred souls, right?"

He shrugs, as if he does not care. As if he is not afraid. And it is okay, because he has no need to be. I want to comfort him. Tell him he is wrong, but perhaps this is for the best. Let him worry about himself, and what will truly happen can do so without hindrance. He cannot try to save what he does not know needs saving.

My Love. My Hero.

I squeeze his hand and say nothing.

The rest of the drive is silent. When camp comes into view, I want to turn away, to slow down. To prolong the moment.... but the first sun has risen, pinkening the purple sky. Preparations need to be done before the second. There is no more extra time.

There never was extra time.

I steer the rover to the edge of camp, parking it like Evan showed me. I am a good student. He watches me operate the controls with a soft look of pride. A future teacher, basking in the success of his student. I smile at him.

You will have many pupils and accomplish every goal you set, because that is who you are. Who Corin was, before Kahanna...before me.

I wait for him to come around and help me out of the rover, because I want to let him catch me. He lingers as he holds me, then sets my feet on the ground and takes my hand. I laugh and swing our arms between us.

"Are you going to let us walk into camp

like this? What if...what if your nymph sees? Or your mage? Or the witch?"

"So, they'll see." He winks at me.

The camp is awake, soldiers in full uniforms bustle between tents, chatting about victories, laughing with friends, doing calisthenics, practicing with weapons. A few stare at us as we walk past. I think if Evan had been with anyone but me, some may have called out lewd comments. But to these people, I am Maiden Imari, and they should bow and revel.

My chest aches, missing plain Imari. But she was gone centuries ago. She only visited last night, and now, she must leave again.

"Evan Tobias Lauduethe!" The witch's voice is shrill.

"*Hades and Ether*, you *fipping gak mopi*! I will kill you!" The mage sounds scary.

And the thunderous silence that follows must be from the nymph.

Evan grimaces, before turning us both to face his angry court.

I take them in as they argue, these gorgeous people who will have a chance to protect what they so fiercely love. Each other. Their families and friends. Their home worlds. Their people. Because they love how Lenorans cannot. They can be selfless.

And today, so can I.

I clear my throat and place myself in front of Evan, in the middle of the yelling match. The mage is actually smoking, the tip of the dagger she holds in one hand is on fire. The witch glares at me, and if looks were poison, I would die here. The nymph is the calm one. He eyes me stonily and signals to the others to be quiet.

Evan places his hands on my shoulders. I hear him suck in a breath, to speak, to tell them...but I cut him off.

"I have a spell to kill Order. And I need all of you to cast it."

He kisses the top of my head and I record it too, adding it to my mental collection. Of being touched, held, thought dear. Loved by another. I smile as wishes and wants and thoughts of loss fade, because I have all I need here in this moment. "We only have until second sunrise. Come with me."

FRACTIONS

END

THE ORDER'S LAST PLAY
SERIES

ABOUT E. ARDELL

E. Ardell spent her childhood in Houston, Texas, obsessed with anything science fiction, fantastic,  paranormal or just plain weird. She loves to write stories that feature young people with extraordinary talents thrown into strange and dangerous situations. She took her obsession to the next level, earning a Master of Fine Arts from the University of Southern Maine where she specialized in young adult genre fiction. She's a big kid at heart and loves her job as a librarian. When she's not working, she's reading, writing, running writers critique groups, producing a webshow, and even writing fan fiction as her guilty pleasure. Her first YA science fiction novel, THE FOURTH PIECE, was released by 48fourteen Publishing in July of 2016. THE FOURTH PIECE went on to win the bronze medal for YA Science Fiction in The Readers' Favorite Book Awards 2017, Most Promising Series in the Red City Review Book Awards 2017, and to be a finalist for the 2017 RONE Awards for YA Science Fiction/ Paranormal. The sequel to her first book, THE THIRD GAMBIT was released by 48fourteen Publishing in November of 2021. Be on the lookout for Book III, THE SECOND ENDGAME, coming soon.

Follow E. Ardell on Social Media:
Instagram: @E.Ardell_author
Twitter: @E_Ardell
TikTok: @E.Ardell
YouTube: www.youtube.com/eardell
Facebook: www.facebook.com/eardell/
Website: EArdell.com

ACKNOWLEDGEMENTS

I want to thank each and every person who has ever read anything about these characters for me. First and foremost, I thank my sister, Candice, who might know my characters than I do. Second, I thank my best friend forever, Katy, who is my biggest cheerleader. I also want to give a shout out to all the members of my Sunday critique group who have all read bits and pieces, or all, of the short stories included in this book.

The universe of ORDER'S LAST PLAY has so many tales to tell, some short, some long, but I want to share them all. I look forward to putting out more novels and novellas in the future.

Thank you for reading!

Made in the USA
Middletown, DE
18 April 2022

64425326R00104